CONFRONTATION
ACROSS THE RIVER

"Hey, you on the bank!" the outlaw shouted. "Me and my boys has made up our minds. We got a sorta notion to give up. But you're going to hafta do what we want, or we won't make no kinda deal a'tall! We'll shoot it out!"

All of the men in the posse were now moving toward the water's edge. As she and Ki followed them, Jessie noticed that all of them carried their rifles. From the expressions on their faces most of them were prepared to start shooting.

Barney O'Connor pushed to the front of the group as the men walked toward the river.

"All right, we'll listen," O'Connor called through cupped hands. "What've you got to say?"

"We talked it out," the killer's spokesman replied. "And we're ready to give in."

"Then start toward shore and hold your guns up over your heads while you're coming in!" O'Connor commanded.

"Not so fast, mister!" the outlaw replied. "We don't trust you any more'n you trust us . . ."

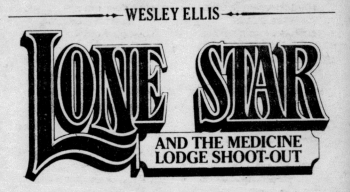

WESLEY ELLIS

LONE STAR

AND THE MEDICINE LODGE SHOOT-OUT

JOVE BOOKS, NEW YORK

LONE STAR AND THE MEDICINE LODGE SHOOT-OUT

A Jove book/published by arrangement with
the author

PRINTING HISTORY
Jove edition/March 1989

ISBN: 0-515-09960-0

Jove Books are published by The Berkley Publishing Group,
200 Madison Avenue, New York, New York 10016.
The name "JOVE" and the "J" logo
are trademarks belonging to Jove Publications, Inc.

PRINTED IN THE UNITED STATES OF AMERICA
10 9 8 7 6 5 4 3 2 1

★

Chapter 1

"Look out, Ki!" Jessie shouted. "Behind you!"

Jessie was riding in front of the small bunch of steers, and Ki was behind them. He'd seen from a distance that some of the steers were about to separate from their fellows. The laggard animals, about a dozen of them, were straggling in a strung-out line and moving more slowly then the main bunch. Jessie noticed the stragglers at almost the same time, and she'd gestured toward the little herd with its ragged straggling pigtail.

Ki had nodded, and they'd toed their mounts to a faster gait to get the strays into the herd and bunch the cattle again. Both of them knew that small isolated bunches of cattle made extra work for the wranglers who would be going out the following day to begin what the ranchers called "the gathers," the job of consolidating small herds into one main herd during the annual roundup.

Suddenly and for no reason that either Jessie or Ki could

1

make out, the steers in the laggard line turned away from the herd and started to scatter and run. When Jessie and Ki saw the cattle beginning to take off in different directions they did not even have to exchange glances. Both of them knew what to do and they started at once to gather the strung-out animals.

Wheeling Sun into a slanting course that would take her far enough away from the cattle to avoid spooking them, Jessie began galloping at an angle that would enable her to turn her mount and stop them. When Ki saw the direction in which she was moving, he turned his own horse in the opposite direction. Their moves put the fleeing steers between them.

Thanks to Sun's great speed and stamina, Jessie reached the spot for which she'd been heading and reined in. Then she turned Sun and sat in the saddle motionless for a moment while gauging the speed of the moving steers and choosing the best course to take in chousing them into a compact bunch again.

Ki made the necessary matching moves. He guided his sturdy cow pony on a line that allowed him to intercept the most distant of the herd-jumpers. The first group of the would-be strays turned and reversed their course when they saw Ki cutting in front of them. Now Ki had the most difficult job of the effort he and Jessie were making. He turned his pony and rode back and forth in front of nearest strays, forcing them to turn and retreat. Then he spurred to a gallop again and circled behind them to the next small group. The motion of his horse moving back and forth in front of the confused animals had the desired effect. These steers also began to retreat, moving toward those which Jessie was now dominating.

Ki quickly narrowed the arc in which he was riding, and

his movements forced the straying bunch of steers into a small compact group with those being held by Jessie. Within a quarter of an hour after the steers had begun to stray, they were in a small compact bunch between Jessie and Ki and the main herd, which was still moving slowly in the direction of the range fence.

Jessie and Ki were riding behind the animals now. There was a distance of perhaps a hundred yards between them as they kept moving constantly back and forth to keep the steers bunched. Both of them were careful to keep their distance from the small group of strays. They had no desire to spook them again, but several of the animals seemed restless and kept trying to break away from the others.

Ki was wheeling his horse to ride from the head of the bunch to its back. He did not see the tail of one of the animals go up, nor did he hear the scraping of its hooves on the baked earth as the steer lowered its head and started toward him.

Jessie's warning call was lost in the sweeping gusts of the unpredictable Texas prairie wind and in the noises of the cattle. Her voice was drowned by the thudding of the steers hooves as they plodded along on the hard-baked soil and by the blatting protests of the cattle at having their actions controlled by the riders.

Jessie touched Sun's flank with her boot-toe and twitched the reins gently to turn the horse. The big cattle-wise palomino wheeled and started in Ki's direction. Rising in her stirrups and waving with her free hand as she tried vainly to attract Ki's attention, Jessie called again, "Ki! Behind you! Steer coming at you!"

Ki heard Jessie's second warning a few seconds too late to rein his pony aside and avoid the maverick's rush. He did succeed in pulling his horse into the start of a turn. The

3

sharp tip of the charging steer's horn missed Ki's leg and his horse's belly. Its curving length slid into the pocket between haunch and belly, and its massive head struck the cow-pony with a thudding blow that sent the horse to the ground.

When Ki felt the animal toppling, his lightninglike reflexes responded almost automatically. With his hands pushing hard on the high front curve of his range saddle, he lifted himself off the horse's back and threw his legs high.

For the fleeting instant that he needed to get full control of his powerful muscles, he held himself in a hand-stand in spite of the horse's erratic movements after taking the bump of the charging steer. Then, twisting his body to one side, he made a final escape by launching himself with a *yoko-tobi* somersault that brought him to the ground. Ki was still on his feet, but now a dozen yards of open prairie separated him and his horse. The still-moving outlaw steer was whirling to repeat its charge.

By the time Ki touched the ground, Jessie had spurred Sun to within a few feet of him. Like Ki, she understood that the half-wild range steers rarely charged a horse, even when there was a rider in its saddle. But they would invariably rush at a man who was standing on the ground.

Though the disturbance at the rear of the herd had not yet drawn the attention of the other steers, Ki knew, as did all ranchers, the ease with which a herd could be spooked. Over the noise of the blatting cattle he heard the rhythmic thudding of Sun's hooves. He turned as the horse reached him and leaped on to its rump while Jessie toed the big palomino beyond the still undisturbed cattle in the string behind the main herd.

"Thanks," Ki said as he settled on Sun's rump in a more

comfortable posture than had been possible earlier.

Jessie nodded to acknowledge Ki's remark, but her eyes were fixed on the steer that had charged him. Ki joined her inspection of the steer. The animal was moving now in an erratic manner, veering from side to side for a few feet, then stopping to swing its lowered head and toss it aimlessly in midair. Both Jessie and Ki could see its walleyed stare as its horns caught the light of the declining sun.

"There's something wrong with it," Jessie said.

"You're right about that," Ki nodded. "And from the way it's acting my guess is locoweed."

"Oh, surely not, Ki! Father was so careful to have the men grub out every trace of it!"

"This is the part of the range where it was thickest," Ki went on. "And I'm sure the men were careful when they were clearing it out, but that grubbing was done quite a while ago. By now it's pretty likely that the locoweed's sprouted again here and there. Those old roots have had plenty of time to send some shoots above ground again."

Still watching the steer's erratic movements, Jessie nodded again. "I suppose you're right," she agreed. "And from the way it's acting that steer's past saving."

As she spoke, Jessie drew her Colt from its holster and touched Sun's flank with the toe of her boot. The magnificent horse moved slowly toward the staggering steer, which was still tossing its head erratically and blatting now and then. Taking quick aim, she sent a bullet into the locoed creature's brain, then followed it with a safety shot.

For a moment the crazed animal continued on its erratic way, then it stopped and began swaying. After a moment its legs folded and the steer dropped to the ground and lay still.

"It'd be a shame to waste all that good beef," Jessie told

5

Ki. "You bleed the carcass while I go after your horse. I'll have Cookie come out with a wagon tomorrow and pick it up."

Ki nodded. "We can always use fresh meat in the cookshack at this time of the year. Kerr can send a couple of the hands to help Gimpy load the carcass in the wagon. Then they can ride this section and look it over for locoweed."

Jessie reined in beside the steer carcass, and Ki slid off Sun's rump. Drawing his *tanto* from its sheath he made swift, sure cuts with the razor-keen blade. He opened main arteries in the dead steer's neck and hindquarters to let the blood drain and to remove the risk that the poison the blood had absorbed would contaminate its flesh.

Leading Ki's horse, Jessie rode up and tossed Ki the animal's reins. They wheeled and started back toward the Circle Star's headquarters, still several miles away. They rode in companionable silence. There was no need for them to talk, for the companionship the two enjoyed was of long-standing. In the years that had passed since the tragic death of Jessie's father, she and Ki had formed a bond of friendship that required no words to maintain.

They'd taken care of the restless range-wild cattle and were returning through the fast-gathering dusk to the main house. The time they'd spent gathering the cattle herd and moving it to the proper pasture had exhausted what remained of the day. Jessie looked at the sun, which almost touched the rim of the horizon.

"We spent more time chousing those half-wild steers than we'd planned on, Ki," she remarked.

"If you're hinting that we'll be late for supper, you're probably right," Ki replied. "But think how much more we'll enjoy it when we finally get home."

"Oh, I'm not all that hungry," Jessie told him. "What

6

I'm really thinking about is that this is mail day, and all those reports I get each month will be waiting for me after supper."

"I'm sure you'll handle them with your usual speed," Ki smiled. "And think how much better you'll feel after you've gone through them and found that everything's still running right."

"Well, things have been going very smoothly of late," Jessie said. "So if something is wrong this time, I suppose I can take care of it without too much trouble."

They rode on across the gently rolling home range. The compactly grouped buildings of the Circle Star finally came in sight. The buildings were silhouetted against the deep, rich, reddish-purple of the after-sunset horizon. Beyond a small cluster of storage sheds and stables the level horizon was broken by the huge block of the main house. It had been patterned by Alex Starbuck along the lines of the old Spanish adobe haciendas which were commonplace in Texas.

Two stories high and almost square in its shape, the big main house dominated the other buildings. Across an open space from the main house stood the long narrow bunkhouse and the smaller, even narrower cookshack where Gimpy, the Circle Star cook, prepared and served the meals for the hands. Both the bunkhouse and the cookshack windows gleamed brightly in the gathering gloom, and to Jessie's surprise a glow of yellow lamplight also shone through the lower-floor windows of the main house.

"Now, that's odd," Jessie frowned. "Kerr doesn't usually go into the main house unless we're there."

"We're getting back a lot later than we'd planned," Ki said. "Maybe Gimpy carried our supper across from the cookshack. I'm sure the hands must be just about through with their supper by this time."

"I suppose so," Jessie agreed. "And Gimpy likes to get supper over and clean up the cookshack before it gets dark."

By this time they'd gotten close enough to the ranch buildings for the thunking of their horses' hooves to be heard inside the cookshack. The door opened and Gimpy pushed through it. Favoring his badly twisted leg, he limped across to the hitch-rail in front of the main house and stood waiting while Jessie and Ki dismounted.

"Figured I better tell you what's going on, Miss Jessie," the cook said as Jessie stepped away from sun. "You got comp'ny inside, some feller from back East. I was here by myself when he rode in, so I done the best I could to make him feel at home. I hope you don't mind."

"Of course not!" Jessie replied. "Who is he?"

"I disremember his name," Gimpy frowned. "But what he told me sounded all right. Said you'd remember him from one time when you was visiting President Hayes in Washington."

"Goodness, I've met a lot of people the two or three times Lucy and President Hayes were kind enough to entertain me at the White House," Jessie frowned. "And don't know how many I've invited to visit the Circle Star. But I'm sure it's all right, Gimpy. It was thoughtful of you to make him feel welcome."

"Well, I reckoned you'd want me to do that, Miss Jessie. And I redded up the dining room and took him some supper afore I dished up for the hands."

"That was very thoughtful, Gimpy. Thank you," Jessie nodded.

Gimpy went on, "Now, I'll bring you and Ki your supper soon as I can step back in the cookshack and git it. I saved it back for you. It'll just take a minute for me to git it outen the oven."

"That'll be fine," Jessie nodded. She turned to Ki as Gimpy started back to the cookshack and went on, "I hadn't counted on finding company when we got back, Ki, and I can't imagine who it might be."

"There's only one way to find out. Let's go in and see who your guest is."

Ki stepped up to the narrow veranda of the main house as he finished speaking. He swung open the massive paneled door for Jessie and stood aside while she entered. The entryway of the main house was long and narrow, with a door at each end. One of the doors led to the main salon and dining room, the other to the spacious room that had been her father's study. Light flooded through the open door of the big study. After closing the outer door, Ki followed Jessie as she moved down the hall. As he reached the study door he heard her voice raised in surprise.

"Jack Carruthers! This is the last place I'd expect to see you!" she said. "But what a nice surprise! Welcome to the Circle Star!"

"I'm sorry I had to surprise you, Jessie," a man's voice replied. "But there wasn't time for a letter to get here before I would, and I found that a telegram couldn't do it, either."

"We're a bit isolated here," Jessie said. "But—" She broke off as Ki entered the study, then went on, "I'm sure you met Ki when we were in Washington, Jack."

"No," the man said. "I didn't have the opportunity, but I certainly remember his name and what you said about him."

"Then it's time you two got acquainted," Jessie went

9

on. "You've heard me speak of Major Carruthers, Ki. I'd forgotten that you two didn't meet while we were in Washington."

"That was mostly my fault," Ki replied as he shook hands with Carruthers.

Though his eyes seemed impassive, he was taking stock of the officer as he spoke. Even in well-tailored civilian garb, the visitor bore the stamp of West Point in his bearing and stance. Carruthers towered over Ki by almost a head. Unlike the military men who spent most of their time in the field, instead of an office, he was clean-shaven. His light brown hair shone from brushing. His features were neither noteworthy nor striking, but managed to meet a happy medium.

Ki went on, "I visited with some of my countrymen while you escorted Jessie to the President's party. I'm very glad to meet you, Major."

"My sentiments, too, Ki. And please forget that I've got a military rank, let me be just Jack Carruthers." Turning back to Jessie he went on, "Before we drop my military rank, I might tell you that it's not major now. Just before leaving on this mission, I was promoted to lieutenant colonel."

"You should have worn your uniform," Jessie scolded mockingly.

"Not while I travel through the South," Carruthers told her. "Even though the war's been over a long time, bluecoats still aren't popular here. I won't put it on until I get to San Francisco. I'm on my way to the Presidio for my first real tour of duty away from Washington."

"And you went out of your way to visit me," Jessie smiled. "I'm flattered, Jack."

"I haven't—" Carruthers broke off as Gimpy came in.

He was carrying a tray that held the belated supper he'd saved for Jessie and Ki.

"We can talk while Ki and I have our supper," Jessie said. "If you don't mind?"

"Of course not. And if you're not too tired after . . . well, doing whatever you do on a ranch . . . we can visit all night."

Jessie slipped her arms into the diaphanous robe she'd chosen from her armoire and pulled it around her freshly powdered body. Though neither she nor Carruthers had even hinted at what the night might hold for them, the memories of their encounter in Washington had returned to her vividly while she bathed and powdered. She was positive that her guest was anticipating her visit.

She was not disappointed. She took the few steps down the hall and tapped with her fingertips on the door of the room to which she'd shown the army officer. Carruthers opened the door at once, and Jessie stepped inside his room. He was barefoot, wrapped in a brocaded dressing gown. Her first glance told her that he was wearing nothing underneath.

"I was sure you'd be waiting for me," she whispered as he closed the door.

"And I was equally sure you'd be tapping on my door when you knew the time was right," he told Jessie as he took her into his muscular arms.

Then Carruthers bent toward her, and Jessie raised her lips to meet his. They held their kiss, questing tongues entwined. Carruthers' forsook his embrace and let Jessie hold him to her, her arms around his waist. He slid his hands along her silk-clad shoulders.

Jessie could feel him swelling as he slipped her robe

from her shoulders. His hands and, after a few moments, his lips found the rosy buds of her swelling breasts. She freed one of her arms and slipped her hand between their bodies, then slid it down between them until she could grasp his already rigid shaft.

As her hand closed around the throbbing cylinder of warm flesh, Carruthers stopped his hand-caresses and started to lift her. She shook her head.

"Not standing here. The bed's only a step away."

Jessie untied her filmy negligee and let it slip to the floor. She then pushed Carruthers' robe free and let it fall atop her own silken garment. Again, she grasped his rigid shaft.

As her hand closed once again around the bobbing member, Carruthers lifted her and stepped to the bed. Jessie did not release him. As he leaned forward, she fell backward and pulled him with her. While relishing the warmth and weight of his body, Jessie positioned him. He drove into her, a deep full penetration, and she gasped with pleasure as she felt his warm rigid cylinder filling her. She locked her legs around his hips and pulled him to her, sighing as he plunged still deeper.

For a moment they lay without moving, then Carruthers sought her lips as he began to thrust. He moved, at first, with slow measured deliberation. Jessie quickly caught his rhythm and matched it with lifted hips. His deliberate thrusts soon quickened. She began rocking her hips, twisting them from side to side to gain the greatest possible pleasure from their embrace.

After her long abstinence, her sensations mounted to the edge of frenzy sooner than she'd expected. She threw back her head, breaking their long kiss, and gasped, "Now, Jack! Drive now! There'll be a next time soon enough!"

Carruthers speeded his stroking in response to Jessie's plea. Then passion's peak took them and carried them to the height of ecstasy until their urgency was satisfied. They did not talk but lay lax and spent, their bodies sated and limp, as they waited for the next time that Jessie had promised.

★

Chapter 2

"It's too bad your friend couldn't stay longer," Ki told Jessie.

Lieutenant Colonel Carruthers had boarded the westbound train by way of the observation platform on the last car. As the train pulled away Jessie and Ki had stood beside the tracks waving at him until they could no longer see him clearly. Now their recent guest was well-started on the last leg of his trip to San Francisco, while Jessie and Ki were almost at the halfway point of their ride back to the Circle Star.

"Yes," she nodded. "Jack is good company. But he's due to report for duty at the Presidio in four days."

"Perhaps it's just as well," Ki said. "Having company during busy times like the gathers and the roundup can be a bit inconvenient."

"Only another rancher could understand that, Ki," Jessie nodded. "Most people don't realize that ranchers are

14

like the nursery rhyme woman, their work is never finished."

"I've never learned your country's nursery rhymes, but I can understand what you mean," Ki said. "As soon as we get back, I've got to finish getting ready for the roundup."

Jessie smiled as she patted the bulging mail sack that hung from her saddlehorn. "And I've got a new sack of mail to add to the one I didn't have time to open yesterday."

During the remainder of their ride back to the ranch they had very little more to say. They reined in at the main house, and Jessie lifted the mail sack from her saddle horn before Ki led the horses to their corral.

"You go ahead with whatever you'd planned to do," she said. "I'm going to whack away at the mail."

In the spacious study that Alex Starbuck had planned for his own use at the ranch, Jessie settled back into the big leather-upholstered easy chair that had been her father's. It still held a faint aroma of the special blend of pipe tobacco that he'd favored.

She opened the mailbag that the hands had brought from the station the day before and dumped it on the table that stood within easy reach of the chair. Then she added the contents of the second mailbag. She sighed when she looked at the heap on the table. She recognized most of the envelopes. They were from the various company managers who were responsible for supervising the day-to-day operations of the expansive Starbuck enterprises that were scattered from New York and Boston to San Francisco and Los Angeles.

"I guess I should've suggested to Ki that he stay and help me go through all this," she sighed aloud. "But he's got his own jobs to do, just as I have."

With that small consoling thought, Jessie picked up the letter-opener and began opening envelopes. Going through the reports of the managers who handled day-to-day operations of the far-flung Starbuck holdings was a job that Jessie had never learned to enjoy. It was one that she handled with her usual quiet competency as an obligation to the hundreds of people whose livelihood depended on the Starbuck enterprises.

When the bullets of hired killers ended her father's busy life, Jessie was still attending finishing school in the East, and had only the sketchiest idea of the vast extent of his holdings. Even though at that time, she was aware of his stature as a giant in the American industrial world.

Ki had been with Alex for several years at the time of the industrialist's assassination. Under Alex's guidance, he'd gained a penetrating knowledge of the many business enterprises that made up the Starbuck holdings. He continued to serve Jessie as he had served her father, for the Oriental custom that bound master and helper together for a lifetime had played a large part in his early upbringing.

Alex Starbuck had been a self-made man. From the start of his business career with a small shop on the San Francisco waterfront dealing in Far Eastern imports, Alex had expanded into general trade in the Orient. His fortune had been founded on the exporting of American products to the huge Chinese-Japanese market and importing of vast quantities of Oriental products into the United States.

Within a relatively short time, he'd bought a cargo ship to carry his own goods. Soon after his initial venture in handling his own shipping, he'd had trouble getting delivery of more modern vessels from the booming East Coast shipyards and had gone into shipbuilding. This had led him to buy timberlands that could assure him of an unfailing supply of planking, tall masts and sturdy spars. He'd built one vessel, then a second and a third, and others followed in quick succession until he could not only supply his own needs but also build vessels for other traders.

Branching out from ocean shipping, Alex had expanded into making steel not only for ships, but also for railroads. His foundries led him into mining and a bit later into the burgeoning railroad-building industries.

To finance his expanding enterprises, Alex had been drawn into banking and later into brokerage. Eventually, his financial holdings were as widespread and profitable as his other ventures. At a relatively early age, Alex Starbuck had become one of the wealthiest and most influential men in America.

By the unforeseen chance of a mortgage forfeiture, Alex had become the owner of a vast tract of land in west Texas. On his first visit to inspect his newly-acquired property, he'd become enchanted with the peaceful isolation the area promised. He'd created the Circle Star Ranch on the un-tamed prairie. He'd married late in life, and after the un-timely death of the beautiful wife, he'd made the ranch his home during the intervals between his visits to his other extensive holdings. Here Jessie had grown up to young womanhood.

Alex Starbuck's rise to prominence and power had not gone unnoticed abroad. Unscrupulous industrialists and fi-nanciers in both Europe and the Far East had formed a secret cartel that had the objective of siezing control of America's industrial wealth by any means, including stealth and murder. Alex had refused an invitation to join the cartel. Instead he'd battled its sinister minions until a hired gunman of the cartel brought his life to an end in a hail of bullets.

Ki's early life had been spent in a different manner. He was the son of one of Alex's close friends, an American in Japan, and a Japanese woman from one of the country's ancient noble families. Disowned by her family for having married a foreigner, Ki's mother had died penniless.

Shunned by his mother's family, Ki had spent his early years on the mean streets of the Orient. He'd lived from hand to mouth, running errands and doing other small menial jobs as he struggled to survive. Then, in his early youth, good fortune came his way. He'd drawn the attention of an aged samurai, Hirata, who in his own younger days had also been banished by an austere family.

At the time of his banishment, Hirata had possessed one skill, that of unarmed combat, and had opened a *do* to instruct others in the developing art. Struck by the parallel between his own life and Ki's, Hirata took Ki into his home as a foster son. There he'd passed on to Ki the secrets and skills that he'd spent his lifetime mastering, until the young Ki's mastery of combat crafts matched his own.

At the time Ki was a vagabond freelance fighter, Japan and its newly conquered province of Korea were in turmoil. Ki moved from the private army of one samurai to another, a freelance mercenary, selling his fighting skills to the highest bidder. It was a bitter and dangerous life, and as he matured, Ki realized that he must change his ways in order to survive.

While still a child, Ki had heard of Alexander Starbuck. In his desperation to find a new way of life he scraped together the money needed to buy passage on a ship to America. After landing in San Francisco, he'd looked up Alex and sought his advice on the best means to survive in

America. Impressed by the young man's intelligence and fighting skills, and because of the friendship between himself and Ki's dead father, Alex had hired him as a personal companion and bodyguard.

From the moment of his mentor's death, Ki blamed himself for having been away from Alex's side when the cartel's hired gunmen struck. With the tactful skill that was part of his Oriental heritage, Ki trod the narrow line of being Jessie's companion, protector and friend, without interfering in her business decisions or stepping into her private life.

Jessie matched Ki in understanding. He taught her more than a little of the unarmed combat skills he'd acquired, and she had already learned much about Far Eastern thinking from the wise old former geisha who had attended to her after the untimely death of her mother. Even before Jessie had become a student in the fashionable Eastern seminary for young ladies, the old geisha had taught Jessie the sexual arts of the Japanese Pillow Book as well as the *prajna* and *karuna* philosophy on which Zen is based.

Following her father's untimely death, Jessie and Ki had battled the sinister European cartel that had been trying to wrest Alex's industrial empire away. The fight waged by Jessie, with Ki at her side, had been long and exhausting, but victory had been their final reward.

During the period of peaceful calmness that followed, Jessie had been able to enjoy an extended period of relative leisure for the first time since Alex's death. By choice, she'd spent more and more of her time at the Circle Star. There had, however, been sudden spurts of action to interrupt the placid life that the vast size and isolation of the ranch made possible.

Jessie was going through the stack of routine reports,

scanning each one quickly and picking out its core features with the skill experience had taught her. In addition to the reports, there was the usual gaggle of begging letters from the genuinely needy as well as the confidence artists. Jessie's hands moved from one piece of mail to another as she separated the wheat from the chaff with a single quick glance.

She'd almost finished going through the stack. Then she picked up an envelope that she hadn't noticed earlier when she was sorting the mail to separate her own letters from the few that were addressed to the ranch hands. The postmark on the envelope showed it had been mailed at Medicine Lodge, Kansas, and that rang a tiny bell in Jessie's memory. She opened the envelope and read the short message on the one page letter the envelope contained:

Dear Miss Starbuck:

I guess you have heard by now about my father's death, since he passed away almost a year ago.

I haven't written you about the promissory note that he gave Mr. Starbuck when he was opening up the bank here, because the note has just come due.

Since my father's death, I've decided that I don't want to continue being a banker. Right now, I'm selling the bank to Mr. E. W. Payne, and he's going to pay me in a few days. Please, don't worry about the note being a little bit past due. I'll send you the money as soon as Mr. Payne pays me.

Yours truly,
Blaise Caldwell

A frown rippled across Jessie's face as she put the letter aside with the few others that she'd reserved to discuss with Ki after they'd had their supper.

Jessie and Ki were sitting in the big study that had become her favorite room, just as it had been her father's. Ki had kindled a small blaze in the fireplace, more to add a cheerful touch to the evening than to banish the usual after-sunset chill. Now, the big fireplace held only a bed of dying coals.

"We only have one more letter that I want to ask you about," Jessie told him. She picked up the envelope with the Medicine Lodge postmark on it and passed it over to him. "What do you remember about the deal Alex made when he loaned the money to help finance this bank?"

Ki took out the single page that the envelope contained and looked at it quickly. Then he said, "I remember that he made the loan only because Kent Caldwell was one of his oldest and closest friends."

Jessie nodded. "Yes, that sounds like him. Alex was a good judge of character. If he trusted a man, he'd go all the way to help him."

"At the time, Caldwell wanted Alex to be his partner in the bank deal," Ki went on. "But Alex had so many irons in the fire that he didn't feel he ought to add an involvement in a bank that depended on a new town like Medicine Lodge."

"Alex must've thought a bank there would be profitable, though, or he wouldn't have loaned Kent Caldwell the money needed to finance it," Jessie said thoughtfully.

"At the time Alex made that loan, Kansas hadn't been a state too long, and it was growing very fast," Ki said. "But at the moment, I don't remember just how much money was involved."

"I do, because I looked in the ledger to find out. Alex loaned his friend $250,000. If the interest on the loan isn't paid each year, it's added to the principal and due when the note is paid off. Blaise Caldwell owes more than $350,000, Ki."

"That's quite a bit of money to come up with in one chunk, even for a banker," Ki frowned.

"If you want to be precise about it, the note is actually overdue," Jessie replied. "But I don't intend to press Kent Caldwell's son for payment."

"You can't carry the note yourself forever, Jessie," Ki pointed out.

"I don't intend to, Ki. It wouldn't be good business to do that. But right now we've got more than enough to keep us busy here at the Circle Star, with the gathers, the roundup, and the market herd to ship. If I haven't heard from Caldwell by the time work slacks off here at the ranch, I'll be looking at that note again."

With a rasp of its rusty rollers and the clanking of its latch, the door of the last cattle car slid shut. The blatting of the steers while they were being choused up the loading chute had already died away. Once they were crowded with their kind in the slat-sided car they settled down. Jessie turned to Ki, a smile of satisfaction on her face.

"That's the end of the market herd for this year," she said. "Now we can go back to the Circle Star and enjoy doing nothing for a few days."

"And after that?"

"Being here at the station has reminded me that we need to make a little trip. After we've rested a day or two, suppose we start clearing away some unfinished business."

"Medicine Lodge and Alex's loan to the banker?"

"Of course. That big unpaid note keeps popping into my mind. It's been almost a month since Blaise Caldwell's letter, and I haven't heard anything from him in spite of his promise."

"More than one-third of a million dollars is a sizeable amount of money," Ki nodded.

"Yes. As long as we're here at the station, let's see how much of a problem we'll have getting to Medicine Lodge on the train. Then when we decide we've rested enough, we'll go there and see for ourselves just what the situation is."

Medicine Lodge on a cloudy Kansas morning looked anything but attractive as Jessie and Ki approached it. Most of its houses were unpainted, and their sides were weathering to the dull gray of unpainted lumber, a gray that matched the rain-threatening sky. The little stream, which they'd gotten an occasional glimpse of beyond the town, looked as gray as the few scattered houses and barns, which now rose a bit more than a mile ahead of them.

From the distance that still lay between Jessie and Ki and the settlement, they could see no apparent pattern in the location of the houses that formed it. They saw no straight streets to align the dwellings into orderly rows or squared blocks; the houses simply straggled willy-nilly across the flat prairie.

As nearly as Jessie and Ki could make out, Medicine Lodge had no features to distinguish it from other similar towns they'd encountered elsewhere on the western prairie. Only within the past few years had the prairie been cleared of Indians and opened for settlement.

There seemed to be only one real street in town. It was a continuation of the ragged dusty trail that Jessie and Ki had been following from Wichita. The river west of Medicine Lodge's buildings was the first running water they had seen since splashing their horses across a somewhat larger stream near the end of their first day's ride from Wichita.

With the caution that had become an ingrained habit during their days of almost constant threat from vicious enemies, Jessie and Ki reined in before they reached the first of the straggling houses. They sat without talking as they surveyed the terrain ahead.

Flanking a few of the scattered houses that lay between them and the town were kitchen gardens beginning to show the first signs of greening. Beyond the formless little community on the west, as well as beyond the river to both the north and the south, pale green shoots of sprouting wheat covered the landscape and hid the ocher soil.

Beyond the scattered houses, there were more substantial buildings. It was obvious that these made up the core of the town, its business district, even though the buildings were few in number.

Despite the distance that still lay between them and the heart of Medicine Lodge, Jessie and Ki could see a dozen structures of cut stone, pale red brick, or neat clapboard siding. As few and widely-spaced as the commercial establishments were, they gave Medicine Lodge the semblance of being a town.

"What on earth could Alex's friend have been thinking of, to build an expensive building for a bank in a place like this?" Jessie frowned as she turned to Ki from the vista ahead.

"We've seen the same thing before, Jessie," Ki reminded her.

"Yes, of course, but that was farther west. The towns there are certain to grow."

"I suppose this one was, too," Ki said. "Remember, it hasn't been too long since the Indians, who considered this

24

to be holy ground, were resettled south in the Indian Nation."

"That was more than ten years ago," Jessie reminded him.

"But the place doesn't have any promise of gold to bring people here to settle."

"Yes, I suppose that does make a difference," Jessie agreed. "But now that I see Medicine Lodge, I can understand why Kent Caldwell was never able to repay the money Alex loaned him. He expected the town to grow, like those farther west did during the Gold Rush."

"But it didn't," Ki nodded. "I suppose people who were moving west were mostly farmers hoping they'd strike gold, and just passed here in a hurry on their way to the diggings."

"That must've been how it was," Jessie agreed. She toed her horse into motion. "Well, even though I'm pretty sure what we're going to find when we go to the bank, we'd better go on into town. But I'm sure this is going to be a wasted trip."

"From what we're looking at now, I'm inclined to—" Ki broke off as the report of a shot sounded ahead, quickly followed by several more. He went on, "That's either somebody settling a barroom brawl or outlaws at work."

"Whichever it is, we'd better get to those houses ahead so we'll have a place to duck behind if trouble comes our way," Jessie said.

Past dangers had shown both Jessie and Ki the need for quick reactions when shooting started. They wasted no more time but spurred ahead toward the nearest building that offered shelter.

★

Chapter 3

While Jessie and Ki were moving toward their new objective no more shots came from the town ahead, but the weather that earlier had been confined to the threat of a gray cloud-obscured sky was beginning to fulfill its promise. The clouds had been with them since daybreak, but the first warning they'd gotten that the storm they'd anticipated was real was being given now in the form of good-sized raindrops that had begun to fall in loud spattering showers.

Jessie glanced at the sky and shook her head. She twisted in her saddle and began pulling at the thongs that held her rolled-up slicker behind its cantle.

"Those clouds ahead are heavier than ever now and moving this way, Ki," she said. "We're going to get wet."

Ki had already seen the sky and was following Jessie's example. He was also riding twisted in the saddle while he freed his own slicker from the saddle strings. He said,

"We've been rained on enough to know that it's not going to melt us."

Jessie did not reply at once. She was busy pulling on the yellow oilskin raincoat that she'd finally gotten free. The real rain was reaching them now. Giant-size drops, which were driven by sudden wind-gusts, struck almost as hard as stones. To the north and to the west, the horizon was lost behind the heavy veil of the rain-sheets.

With her raincoat in place and buttoned to the collar, Jessie took a quick glance at the scattered buildings they were approaching. They were only a short distance from a big ramshackle barn. It stood isolated. There was no house near it, which was not an uncommon sight in the wide belt of Western prairie that was being taken over by wheat-farmers. Many of them followed the northern pattern of building only a barn on their wheat acres and living in a house in town.

"This rain looks like it's going to keep falling a while, Ki," Jessie said. "And it's heavier than we expected. Maybe it would be a good idea to head for that big barn over there and shelter in it."

"If it keeps up this way it'll soak us regardless of our slickers," Ki agreed. "Let's try the barn."

During the few minutes required for them to reach the big rambling barn, they heard no more shooting from town ahead. When they found the barn's doors yawning open, they guided their mounts inside and reined in. The thudding of raindrops on the roof was loud in their ears and reminded Jessie of the shots they'd heard a few moments earlier.

"That shooting we heard must've been cowboys letting

off steam," Jessie suggested. "Whoever it was must've wasted enough shells to satisfy himself."

"Or'run out of ammunition," Ki added.

"Of course, it could've been a saloon brawl, or an argument over a card game, or some sort of private feud that boiled over," Jessie went on. "But thank goodness it's not our affair. You know, Ki, after being a target for so many years, I still can't get used to the fact that I'm not one any longer."

"Those shots could've meant almost anything, Jessie," Ki pointed out. "But as you so aptly put it, it's not our affair, so there's no need for us even to think about them."

"It doesn't look like we've got the rain to think about any more, Ki. That big downpour that we were worrying about has passed over and gone. We can go on into Medicine Lodge now."

Delaying their start only long enough to slip out of their slickers and roll them to replace them on their saddle-cantels, Jessie and Ki toed their horses ahead. They rode for the center of the little town where the houses and buildings stood in a thicker cluster. They reached a point where the random windings of the road ended and began to resemble a street. The thoroughfare became straight instead of meandering, and the shabby cabins they'd been passing were replaced by houses, then by stores.

By this time, the rain had tapered off to a few occasional spatterings. But the heavy blue-black clouds that had been so threatening were still visible beyond the town. The air, which had been like a gray veil less than a quarter of an hour earlier, was clear and fresh.

As they drew closer to the cluster of buildings that formed the core of Medicine Lodge, Jessie and Ki could see an excited crowd milling around one of the three or

28

four cut-stone buildings, which rose above the smaller wood-framed stores and offices that lined the short street.

"I have an idea that we've been guessing in the dark about those shots we heard," Ki said, nodding toward the clumps of people in the street ahead.

"Yes, and I'm getting a hunch that we might be more than casually interested in what happened here, Ki," Jessie said. "That building where the crowd's thickest is the town bank."

"That it is," Ki agreed. "And if your hunch is right we won't have to wait very long before we find out what's happened."

Within the next few minutes, they got close enough to read the painted legend above the wide double doors of the cut-stone building. The legend read MEDICINE VALLEY BANK.

"There can't be more than one bank in a little place like this," Jessie told Ki. They reined in at the edge of the crowd that was milling around in the street.

"Of course not," Ki nodded. He pointed at the store across the street from them. "There's a hitch-rail. Let's find out what we can, then we'll decide what we want to do."

Their horses hitched, Jessie and Ki started weaving their way across the slippery muddy street. They dodged between the group of spectators who were shifting restlessly in front of the bank building. The few words that they heard as they made their slow progress toward the bank did little to give them a clear picture of what had actually happened.

Pushing through the noisily chattering crowd, they reached a spot where only a few onlookers stood between them and the building. Here a dozen or so men had clustered into a knot a few feet away from the bank's hitching-post. Their heads were close together, and they were engaged in a low-voiced discussion. Jessie stopped beside a trio of men who were trying to hear what the small bunch of men in front of the bank's closed doors were saying.

"Can you tell us what happened?" she asked.

"Nobody knows much for sure about anything yet, lady," one man replied. "Except that the bank's likely been held up. I heard some talk that the banker and his cashier was shot, but nobody seems to be sure except that bunch of fellows talking to Barney O'Connor over there."

"Then we'd better go talk to O'Connor and his friends, Ki," Jessie said. She wasted no time, but headed for the tightly-knit group of men standing directly in front of the bank's doors. Ki followed her.

"Damn it, there ain't but three or four of 'em!" O'Connor was saying when Jessie and Ki got within earshot of the huddled group. "What we've got to do is put a posse together and go after 'em! Tracking ain't going to be hard on wet ground!"

"If it don't come a big downpour and wash out the tracks," one of the men put in.

"I say we go find the constable first," another volunteered quickly. "We sure ain't the law here!"

"Hell, Sam Denn ain't anywheres close or he'd be here by now!" O'Connor retorted. "Anyways, we don't need him to put a posse together."

"Anybody know where Sam's at?" another of the men asked. He raised his voice and turned to repeat his question to the onlookers huddled in the lightly-spattering rain. A few shook their heads, but no one answered.

"All we know is that he doesn't seem to be anywhere around town," O'Connor said. "If Sam was anyplace close enough to've heard what's happened, he'd be standing here with us by now."

"It'd be more legal-like if he was with us. What if we catch up to them outlaws and get into a shoot-out," the man who'd suggested finding the constable objected.

"We won't get anywheres close to 'em unless we saddle up and take after 'em right away," O'Connor pointed out.

"I say Barney's right," one of the group agreed.

"And so do I," Jessie broke in.

Her words were followed by an especially loud thunderclap from behind the lowering rain clouds that were still occasionally loosing brief flurries of tiny raindrops. The men whose conversation Jessie had broken into stood staring at her while the rumbles were dying away. Then O'Connor spoke.

"I admire your sentiments, ma'am," he said. "But this is men's business."

"It happens to be my business as well," Jessie retorted crisply. "My name is Jessica Starbuck. My father loaned Kent Caldwell the money he needed to start this bank. That loan still hasn't been repaid, so I suppose you might say that I'm one of the bank's owners."

"You're Alex Starbuck's girl?" one of the men standing near O'Connor asked.

"As I've already told you," Jessie said. Her voice was not loud, but held a steely firmness.

"Damned if—" the man who'd questioned Jessie began, then stopped short and went on, "Excuse my cussing, ma'am. It just sorta slipped out, you taken me by surprise."

"I've heard all the words before," Jessie told him.

"Well, ma'am, what I begun to say was that I knowed your daddy, and I've heard him talk about you, how proud

31

he was of you. Maybe you heard him mention me a time or two. I'm Arch Kettleman. Me and Alex Starbuck got acquainted up in the Yukon Territory, and that was a long, long time ago. While he was getting to be such a big muckety-muck with stores and shipyards and banks and such, I settled down here in Indian Territory to farm and loaf."

"I remember Alex telling me about how you two tried to cook a seal once, when you'd run out of food," Jessie said.

"You're Alex's girl, all right, then," Kettleman agreed. "Now, you ain't what I'd call a spitting image of him, but the way you talk . . . well, that's just the way your daddy did."

"I've been told that before," Jessie smiled.

Turning to the spectators the man who'd questioned Jessie went on, his voice raised to reach to the edges of the crowd. "You don't need to worry about this little lady," he said. "All of you know me, and all of you know that me and Alex Starbuck was good friends. I'll vouch for Miss Jessie any day!"

"Well, Miss Starbuck, if I had any doubt about you before, I certainly don't have now," O'Connor said. "These other fellows here are Lee Bradley and Charley Taliaferro and Tom Doran. And this one by me here is Vern Lytle."

As the men in the group heard their names they nodded to Jessie, but none of them spoke more than a mumbled word or two of greeting.

"Now, I'm real glad to make your acquaintance, Miss Starbuck," O'Connor said. "But I still say going after those mean outlaws is no job for a woman, irregardless of who you are. Why, if—"

He stopped short and gulped when Jessie drew her Colt with a swift motion that would have beaten most professional gunmen and sent a slug thunking into one of the posts that supported the hitch-rail, fifteen feet away.

"Does that change your mind, Mr. O'Connor?" she asked.

For a moment O'Connor did not reply. Then he said slowly, "Well, I'd say you've got a real fine hand with a gun, Miss Starbuck. But it don't exactly change my mind."

"I didn't join you men to put on a shooting exhibition," Jessie told him. "But if you still object to me—and Ki as well, of course—riding with the posse you've suggested —" She broke off as Kettleman and Taliaferro spoke at almost the same moment.

"Don't take this lady for an acorn calf, Barney," Kettleman told O'Connor. "Not if she's her daddy's girl."

"Let her come along, Barney," Taliaferro put in, his words following Kettleman's by only a split-second.

"Now, wait just a minute!" Doran put in. He turned to Jessie and asked, "Are you sure you're up to traveling alongside of us, Miss Starbuck?"

"I'll manage to hold my own," Jessie replied. "And Ki will be with me, of course."

"That's your Chinee friend?" Doran asked.

"Japanese, if you wish to be exact," Ki said quickly. "And I have been with Jessie on much more difficult rides than chasing a handful of bank robbers. You will make no mistake in allowing us to go with you. And if you do not form your posse, I'm sure that Jessie and I will go after the outlaws ourselves."

"Of course," Jessie added. She spoke calmly, but there was a conviction in her voice that registered even on the two men who'd been dubious.

Doran spoke slowly as he said, "Well, it looks like I'm outvoted. All right, Miss Starbuck. You and your friend can come along with us, but I sure hope you got sense enough to duck if bullets start flying."

"You are going to go after the bank robbers, then?" Jessie asked.

"You can just bet we are!" O'Connor assured her.

"Good. Ki and I will be ready the minute you've got your posse assembled," Jessie said. Then she added, "There is one favor I'd like to ask of you, Mr. O'Connor."

"Ask away, ma'am. Anything reasonable."

"It's going to take you a little while to get a group ready to ride," Jessie pointed out, then added quickly, "Since for all practical purposes, I'm one of the owners of the bank, I'd like to take a look inside."

For a moment O'Connor did not answer. When he did speak, it was obvious that he was choosing his words carefully. He asked Jessie, "You've got some reason for wanting to go in there, I guess?"

"I'm not trying to satisfy some morbid curiosity," Jessie assured him. "For one thing, I'd like to make sure that the vault is locked and . . . well, take a look around for anything that might be out of order."

"Miss Starbuck, there's one dead man and another dying behind those doors. They're not very pretty to look at," O'Connor protested.

"I've seen such men before," Jessie said calmly. "Besides, Ki will be going in with me."

"Well. . . . I don't see that I've got any right to say yes or no, but everybody's acting like I'm in charge of things," O'Connor answered slowly.

"I'm only interested in checking to be sure the vault is locked," Jessie said.

"Like I told you, the inside's not something you'd want to look at," O'Connor warned Jessie for the second time.

"Poor old George Gephart's body is laying propped up against the vault and Payne's sprawled out in the middle of the floor. Like I said, it's not real nice to look at."

Jessie nodded. "I don't intend to disturb anything. And Ki and I will be ready to ride as soon as you can get your friends together."

"And we better be cutting a shuck, too, or the robbers will get away from us," O'Connor exclaimed.

He turned back to the men surrounding them. Already a few of them had vanished, but eight or ten remained.

"Are you aiming to take charge of things?" Doran asked.

"Well, somebody's got to, and Sam Denn still hasn't shown up," O'Connor replied. "Anybody objecting?"

For a moment none of the men spoke, then Taliaferro said, "It looks like you're elected, Barney. It just makes sense, you're the only one of us who's ever been a lawman."

"All right, then," O'Connor nodded. "Go and get your horses saddled up. All of you bring rifles, pistols, too, I guess you've got both. Don't waste any time. The quicker we get after those murdering skunks, the better."

As the men in the little group began to scatter, Jessie stepped up to the door of the bank. A few men in the crowd that had kept their distance from the group which formed the posse began edging closer as she opened the door. Motioning for Ki to move quickly, Jessie stepped aside to let him enter the bank, then quickly followed him inside and closed the door behind her.

O'Connor's sketchy description of what they would find had been accurate. The bodies of two men lay on the lobby floor. Payne was sprawled on his back on the floor in the center of the wide rectangular room with two men attend-

35

ing his wound. Gephart lay at the back, propped up in a sitting position against the wall near the burnished steel door of the vault.

A short-barrel Colt New Line Revolver was visible on the floor next to the wounded man, and his face was distorted and covered with blood. The corpse propped up against the vault's wall was that of an elderly man, partly bald, coatless but wearing a vest. His face was as peaceful as though he was alive and staring across the room at Jessie and Ki. However, both his shirt and vest were covered with a massive bloodstain.

"From the way these bodies look, those outlaws started shooting the minute they came through the door," Jessie said to Ki as they stopped just inside the bank lobby and scanned its interior.

"It certainly looks that way," Ki agreed.

Jessie stepped around the extended legs of the man propped against the vault's side and tried the door-lever. It did not move. She turned to Ki and said, "It's still locked, all right. From the evidence, this man by the vault must have thrown the combination before he died.

"My guess is that the robbers were waiting outside for the man on the floor to go into the bank," Jessie went on thoughtfully as she surveyed the interior. "He still has his coat on, so it's easy to figure out that he'd come in from the street."

"That's the way I see it, too," Ki told her. "Then when the outlaws realized what they'd done, they panicked and ran."

"And I suppose are still running," Jessie agreed. "I don't think we need look at anything else, Ki. I've found out what I wanted to know."

"That the vault hadn't been left unlocked?"

"Of course. That was one of the reasons I came inside. I don't doubt that there are some people here in Medicine Lodge who'd take advantage of all the excitement to rob this place. I also wanted to see if we could aid Mr. Payne, but he appears to be well tended. We can go back and join the posse now."

"Yes," Ki nodded. "These men are so involved in trying to save Mr. Payne that they don't even seem to have noticed us. The only thing left to do for him is to hunt down the men who did this."

After Jessie and Ki shut the building's door behind them, she and Ki turned to scan the street. Jessie had expected a crowd to be forming. But a new batch of dark towering clouds was scudding across the gray sky, and apparently the threat of rain had kept the curious at home. Jessie stepped up to Barney O'Connor.

"I've seen all I need to," she said. "Now, Ki and I are ready to ride with you and your posse until we catch up with the crooks who shot those two men inside the bank."

★

Chapter 4

"We'll be moving pretty quick, ma'am," O'Connor said. "All the others except Charley and Vern over there"—he paused long enough to indicate the two men standing beside their horses at the hitch-rail—"had to go get their horses and rifles. Soon as everybody's here, we'll pull out."

"Ki and I can start any time," Jessie told him. "We're traveling light, so we don't need to do anything to get ready, and our horses are rested from the ride here. We can leave as soon as the other men come to join you."

"First thing we've got to do before we set out is to figure which way those killers went when they left the bank," O'Connor frowned. "I've asked everybody I've run into, and nobody seems to've noticed 'em."

"That's odd," Jessie frowned. "Surely there were people on the street here who'd have looked pretty closely at a bunch of strange riders."

"Don't forget that it was raining pretty good right about the time they came into town, Miss Starbuck," O'Connor told Jessie. "When a hard rain like we just had blows into a place as dry as this one generally is, most folks stay indoors."

"That's true," Jessie nodded. "But somebody in town must have been looking out a window and noticed . . ." She paused, frowning thoughtfully. Then she went on, "How many men were there in the gang that intended to rob the bank? Three? Four? Six?"

"That's something else we don't know," O'Connor said. "And there's no tracks that might help us figure it out because the ground all around the stores and the bank here is mostly packed down right hard. Where it's not, there's such a mess of hoof-prints that you can't tell a thing about 'em."

"Have you had any experience in tracking?" Jessie asked.

"Well, I guess you'd call it that. I worked on a ranch once. I was always the one that had to run down the steers that strayed. But that wasn't much of a job, and I haven't done anything like that since I come back here to Kansas."

Ki had been listening to the exchange between Jessie and O'Connor. Now he said, "Perhaps I can help." Facing O'Connor, he went on, "I have some small skill at tracking. The ground will be wet after the rain, and the soft dirt will hold hoof-prints for a long time. If you'd like for me to pick up the trail—"

"I'm glad you offered, Ki," Jessie broke in. "I was just going to suggest that you might find some tracks that would help us in running down those killers. I'll be going with you, of course."

"Suppose we can go now, Jessie, while Mr. O'Connor waits for the other volunteers to return?" Ki suggested. "If we do find the tracks of the killers, we can stay on them and mark the trail for the posse to follow."

"If we're going to have any luck at all, we'd better get started right away, Ki," Jessie suggested. She pointed to the sky, where dark clouds were beginning to form in big roiling masses. "It looks like there's more rain coming."

After he'd glanced at the sky and the new storm clouds that were gathering, Ki nodded and said, "Yes, we'd better get started right away."

Jessie turned back to O'Connor and said, "Nobody seems to have seen the killers when they rode off. Which way do you think they went?"

"I'd guess that they headed for the river," he replied. "There's a lot of brush and some trees in the bottom land, and some pretty long stretches of ground where there's gullies and little canyons they could hide in."

Jessie nodded and said, "Then the best thing is for Ki and me to go ahead while you wait for the rest of your men to get back. When they do, you can lead them to Ki and me."

"I don't reckon you've got any idea where you'll be?" O'Connor asked.

Ki replied instead of Jessie. "We can't be sure," he said. "But we'll start where you suggested, southwest of town, along the river. Jessie and I rode in from the northeast, and we met no riders coming from here. That means the killers must have headed for the broken country along the river."

"Everything you've said sounds sensible," O'Connor nodded. "Now that I think about it, there's two or three likely spots along the river where they might be."

"We'll check them out if you'll tell us about them," Jessie suggested.

"You'll see two or three little canyons between the road

40

and the river. Some of them are shallow, the road cuts right on through them. But it curves around the bigger ones."

"That gives us an idea what to watch for," Jessie nodded. "When you're in strange country, every little bit helps."

Ki looked questioningly at Jessie and asked, "Hadn't we better be moving now?"

"Yes, of course," she nodded. Turning back to O'Connor, she said, "We'll be looking for you to catch up with us."

"We'll start as soon as the men are ready," he said. Then he took a half-step away from Jessie and Ki and called to the two men who were still standing beside their mounts, "Miss Starbuck and Ki are going to scout around, see if they can pick up the trail of those mangy outlaws. You got any ideas?"

"Maybe me and Vern oughta go with 'em," Taliaferro called back. "It's pretty rough country along the river. Lots of brush beds and trees in the brakes. How about it, Vern?"

"I'm game all right. But I think Barney oughta go 'cause he's a better shot, and I oughta stay here and wait for the others to show up," Lytle said.

"Makes sense to me," O'Connor replied. "You wait for the others to come back. I'll go ahead with Miss Starbuck and her man. You and the rest of the boys can start soon as all of 'em get back. It won't take long for you to catch up to us."

Jessie and Ki wasted no more time. They swung into their saddles and, with Taliaferro and O'Connor flanking them, started through town, heading for the faint line of brush that marked the course of the Medicine Lodge River.

Dark clouds still obscured the sky, turning it gray. A thin wind had sprung up, giving the air an unseasonal chill.

41

Before they'd ridden a quarter of mile, the clouds began dropping occasional showers of cold misty rain. The rain was not hard and driving, but a drizzle of tiny drops that stung like needles for a second or two and brought a prickling chill to the skin on the riders' faces and ungloved hands.

By unspoken consent, they stopped riding abreast when they reached the spot where the road narrowed, no more than a quarter of a mile beyond the last scattered houses of Medicine Lodge. Ki kept the lead, his keen eyes scanning the road. Jessie stayed a short distance behind him, Taliaferro and O'Connor rode in the rear.

Though Ki was sure that he could identify the most recent hoofmarks on the uncertain trail, which the road had become soon after they'd gotten beyond the settlement, he soon found that this was impossible. This was not because of his lack of skill, for Ki was a shrewd tracker.

While horseshoes left a clear and distinctive mark on soil that was either wet or dry, the thin mist was not liquid enough really to wet the soil. It did nothing more than dampen the earth's surface and form a thin layer of moisture that was neither dry nor wet enough to be called mud. When the horse lifted its hoof, the damp earth clung to the shoe and was lifted free from the surface, leaving only a dry circular mark with blurred edges that showed the shoe's general shape.

All Ki could do was follow the blurred saucer-shaped impressions that the killers' horses had left. There were times when the trail crossed a rock outcrop, where there were no marks to guide him. It was at one of these outcrops, an expanse of virtually barren stone almost a quarter-mile wide, that the drizzle of fine foglike droplets that had filled the air suddenly became a driving rain. Big drops pelted down out of the lowering sky and rolls of distant thunder rumbled now and then.

Ignoring the downpour, Ki and Jessie zigzagged back and forth across the rocky expanse. Their horses' hooves sent up sprays from the puddles that formed quickly on the broken uneven surface. At last Ki reined in, and Jessie brought her horse to a halt when she reached his side. Taliaferro and O'Connor had stopped while Jessie and Ki were making their zigzag examination and now they moved up and reined in.

"It looks like we've lost their trail completely this time," Jessie told them, as they sat huddled in their slickers in the driving rain, surveying the barren expanse of stone.

"We have," Ki agreed. "And when I rode across this stretch of solid rock to where it ends, there weren't any hoof-prints in either direction."

"Did you go all the way to the river?" Taliaferro asked.

Ki shook his head. "I just rode along the edge of this big outcrop for a few hundred feet on each side of the line of prints we'd been following."

"There's a little canyon between here and the river," Taliaferro went on. "I don't guess you went far enough ahead to run into it?"

Shaking his head, Ki replied. "No. I was more interested in finding their tracks again than in exploring very far."

"That canyon's the first place somebody who knew this part of the country would think to hide in," O'Connor put in. "And there's another canyon up ahead that's pretty much like this one, too. They're both about as deep as a barn is high."

"I'm sure they got this far," Ki said thoughtfully. "But if they went beyond the edge of the outcrop, the rain's washed away their trail. At least, I couldn't find any sign of hoof-prints beyond the rock."

"As long as we're so close to those two canyons, we'd better check both of them out," Jessie suggested. "It seems to me that somebody running away from a couple of murders might very well head for the nearest safe hiding place."

"If that's what we need to do, we might as well try the little one first," Taliaferro said. "It's not very far from where we are now. Ki, you must've been almost near enough to see it when you were scouting toward the river."

"Maybe I turned back too soon," Ki replied.

"If you did, I can understand why," Jessie told him.

She waved to indicate the big stretch of barren rock ahead. The rain was pelting down harder now, and the wet surface of the outcrop glistened like glass in the gray sunless light.

Turning to Taliaferro, she went on, "If you'll ride in the lead and show us where it is, we'll have a look."

"It'll be easier if we go on foot," Taliaferro suggested. "All there is between us and the rim is bare rock, and as wet as it is now the horses would likely slide around too much."

"One of us better stay here and hold 'em, then," O'Connor said. "There's sure not anything to hitch 'em to."

"Suppose you stay," Jessie told him. "If you hear shots, take a chance and let the horses go, then come join us."

"I sure will, Miss Starbuck," O'Connor nodded as he moved from one horse to the next, taking their reins.

With Jessie and Taliaferro using their rifles as batons and occasionally as canes with which to balance themselves, they started moving cautiously across the treacherous stone surface, making sure with each step that their boot soles were planted solidly on the rain-slick rock.

Ki was more surefooted than his companions. Not only were his hands free, while Jessie and Taliaferro were forced to use both hands in gripping their rifles, but his soft sandals adjusted more readily to the slick stone surface than did the wet stiff leather soles on the boots worn by Jessie and Taliaferro.

By now the granite outcrop was awash, almost a half-inch deep in sheening ripples of rainwater. The pelting downpour showed no signs of a let up, and the stone surface slanted downward in the same direction in which they were walking. Soon they could see the jagged edge of the huge rock formation through the thick patter of the raindrops. Though the distance they needed to walk was relatively small, the drop-off seemed to be moving away from them in spite of their steady progress.

They were within a half-dozen careful steps from the rim of the outcrop when the first shot sounded from the canyon. Walking in the lead, Jessie dropped into a crouch, using the butt of her rifle as a brace while she shifted her feet to enable her to hunker down. Ki crouched at the same time Jessie did, but their companion was not as lucky or as cautious. Taliaferro dropped flat, cursing under his breath as he stretched belly-down in the chilly water and it soaked into his clothing.

"Are you all right?" Jessie asked.

"I didn't get hit," Taliaferro replied. "But that slug sure didn't miss me by much."

Ki had not stopped when the shot sounded. He was still edging ahead carefully, hunching down lower than before, his back curving, his shoulders level with his knees. A second shot rang out from the canyon, and the bullet that whistled within an inch or two of Ki's ear sent him craw-fishing backward. Still another shot broke the air from below, but Ki had already gotten to a point where the lead missed him by a foot.

"I hope you're all right, too, Ki," Jessie said.

"I didn't get hit," Ki answered. "And I got close enough to take a quick look into the canyon. It's not very deep, but there's a lot of brush growing on the bottom. I couldn't see very well through the bushes and this rain, but there are horses down there and men with them, of course."

"We've run the outlaws to earth, then," Jessie said.

"I'd say that's a pretty safe bet, Jessie," Ki agreed.

"Then all we've got to do is keep them holed up there until we decide on the best way to get them out," Taliaferro observed. "But if this rain keeps up, it might be a real job to scramble our nags over the rocks to get at them."

"That's right," O'Connor nodded. "One thing we better be thinking on, though. As I recall, that canyon has only one opening down by the road. The killers could just go back down the open end and escape."

"Not if one of us is guarding it," Jessie said. "Reining a horse up that slope would be a slow job. They'd know what easy targets they'd be."

"Maybe it's not as big a job as we might think," Ki told her. "I could see the river down at the bottom of that canyon. It's pretty rough and roily, and there's a lot of floating brush on its surface. I'd hate to try reining a horse through it right now."

"Then all we've got to do is keep them holed up!" Jessie exclaimed. "It should be easy enough to do, Ki."

"I think so, too," Ki nodded. "There's enough rain running down into that canyon that they're either going to have to swim or surrender."

46

"Me, I hope they swim!" Taliaferro exclaimed. "Then they'll have to move so slow that we can pick them off like sitting ducks!"

"Whichever way it turns out, we've got them," Jessie pointed out. "If that water keeps rising, it's going to fill the canyon after a while. If they try to swim, they'll be easy targets, sitting ducks, like Taliaferro just said."

"If much more water comes into this little canyon, they won't have any choice," Ki put in. "There's no thick brush up at this end they can use for cover."

"Yes, that's right," Jessie agreed. Then she frowned thoughtfully and went on, "Three of us up here and one with a rifle down by the road is all we need to keep them bottled up now, but what if the rain lets up and the water starts to fall?"

"Jessie's right," Ki agreed. "Things will change if the water stops rising. But we're supposed to have some more help pretty soon. Let's—"

He stopped as a thudding of hoofbeats sounded over the still constant patter of the rain, and then a shout reached them from the road.

"Hold up, fellows!"

Jessie recognized Vern Lytle's voice at once and said, "We're all right now. That's the rest of the posse." Turning in the direction of the road she called, "Here we are! Over here!"

Five or ten minutes of confusion followed as the posse turned their horses and O'Connor crossed the rock outcrop to lead the way. The rain that had been gusting occasionally was now falling steadily and the surface of the huge stone area was almost glass-slick. The confusion did not end until the newcomers dismounted and tethered their horses at the edge of the area where the rock formation surfaced.

O'Connor stopped beside Jessie and Ki. He looked beyond them to the yawning crevasse that split the rain-slick, stony surface. Then he said, "Maybe we better tell them what's been happening before we think about anything else."

"We've got the killers bottled up right now," Jessie announced. "They're in that little canyon, and the water's so high right now that the only way they can get out is to swim."

O'Connor glanced beyond Jessie and looked for a moment at the yellow-red surface of the swirling water, then turned back, a grin on his face.

"I'd think twice about staying down there much longer myself, the way it looks now," he said. "But since we've got all the men we need now, we ought to be able to get the killers out. Chances are they're wetter than we are."

"There are four of them in the canyon, and I'm sure they must've been able to count us when we got here. Now that they can see the reinforcements," Jessie reasoned, "they might surrender."

"It won't do any harm to try," O'Connor told her. Stepping up closer to the rim of the little box canyon, he shouted, "You men down there! We've got you outnumbered about three to one! Be smart and give up, now!"

"Not a chance!" one of the outlaws called in reply. "We're not damn fools enough to go to a necktie party!"

"I promise you there won't be any lynching!" O'Connor shouted in response. "Ride up here to the road with your hands empty and we'll take you back to Medicine Lodge! You'll have a fair trial with a judge and jury!"

"And get strung up by the neck when it's over!" one of

the men in the canyon called back. "Go to hell, whoever you are! We'll stay down here and fight!"

Another of the fugitives in the canyon took up the shouting colloquy. He screamed, "We still ain't heard from no lawman! If you had one up there with you, he'd be doing things by the book. You can't lie to us and get away with it!"

Keeping her voice pitched low, Jessie told O'Connor, "They aren't going to give up, that's pretty clear."

"No. I didn't really think they would," he replied. "But I felt like I had to give them a chance to surrender."

"They're not going to have much choice, if we've got the patience to wait a couple of hours," Ki broke in. "I've been keeping an eye on the water. It's filling up that canyon pretty fast. If we just wait a while, they'll be forced to come out of it and surrender."

"Or try to get to the road and escape," Jessie suggested.

O'Connor shook his head. "No. They wouldn't still be there in the canyon if they thought they had a chance to do that. They'd have been running for the road before now."

"I think he's right, Jessie," Ki agreed.

"Now if there's a chance we can avoid a gunfight, we're better off waiting," Jessie agreed. "And judging by the way the rain keeps coming down, the water will keep on rising for quite a while. But you're the one to make the final decision, Mr. O'Connor."

"Then I say let's wait a little while, at least," he said. "But we'll put guards along the sides of the canyon in case they abandon the horses and try to climb out this way. And to tell you the truth, Miss Starbuck, I'd like to take them without a gunfight. I want to see those dirty killers hanged!"

★

Chapter 5

Jessie nodded in agreement with O'Connor's vehement remark, then she said, "All of us want that, or we wouldn't
be here. But to get back to our situation right now, I hope
you don't mind me making a suggestion."

"Go ahead," O'Connor nodded.

"We need to string out along the rim of the canyon,
between here and the road."

"We do, at that," he agreed. Stepping up to the group
that had arrived, he said loudly, "Let's just make sure none
of those outlaws gets a chance to sneak away."

"Don't worry," Taliaferro responded. "There's enough
of us now to guard both sides of the canyon, like Miss
Jessie said."

"Suppose you tell us where we better go, then," one of
the newcomers suggested.

O'Connor nodded to the speaker before going on. "You
and Vern know the lay of the land in these gypsum hills, so

you two'll help us most by staying right here," he said. "Bradley, you stay here, too. That leaves the rest of you to go back to the road and come down along the other side, where the brush is thicker. Between us, we'll close this canyon up tighter than a fresh bottle of whiskey!"

"One of us better stay up at the head of the canyon," a man in the group suggested. "They might be fools enough to try and make a break back to the road."

"Decide for yourselves where you need to stay," O'Connor told the speaker. "Just don't scatter too much, in case they try to make a break."

"What if they try to break out?" Lowell Clark asked. "Do we shoot 'em, or what?"

"Hell, shooting's too good for 'em!" Howard Martin put in quickly. "I don't know about the rest of y'all, but I want to watch them bastards dangling from a rope!"

A muttering of agreement came from the others. Alec McKinney called, "Let's take 'em alive! Them two fellers they shot was good men!"

"That's settled, then," O'Connor went on. "Don't shoot any of them unless you've got to."

"How many of 'em are we up against?" Wayne McKinney asked.

"So far we've counted just four," O'Connor replied. "But that's not to say we might've missed seeing all of 'em."

"I don't guess it makes much never-mind, but who in hell is them fellers, anyways?" Clark enquired.

"We don't rightly know that, either, because we haven't been able to get a clear look at them yet," O'Connor said. "I don't guess we will, as long as this rain holds out. But just about everybody in Medicine Lodge knows everybody else, so it stands to reason they're out-of-towners."

51

"Likely just some bunch of outlaws on the move," one of the McKinney's suggested.

"Hell, it don't matter who they are or where they come from either," Martin put in. "We'll find that out after we get our hands on 'em. Right now, let's get busy and keep 'em from giving us the slip."

Jessie and Ki had remained unobtrusively in the background while O'Connor was getting the posse organized. Now Jessie stepped up to him and asked, "Is there anywhere in particular you'd like for Ki and me to be?"

"Well, now, Miss Jessie, I don't feel exactly right about asking your and your friend to do anything more," O'Connor replied. "You've already helped us a lot. If you'd like to go back to town—"

"Thank you, no," Jessie broke in. "We started at the beginning of this, and we'd like to stay with you until it's finished."

"But there's too much risk in nasty weather like this. Riding over this slippery rock, you might get hurt!" O'Connor exclaimed.

"Both of us have been hurt before," Jessie smiled. "And I suppose we've both spent enough time on horseback to take care of ourselves in a pinch."

"Jessie's right," Ki agreed. "The idea that we might run into trouble of some sort doesn't bother either one of us."

"I had a hunch you'd insist on sticking around," O'Connor said. "You're a real determined lady, Miss Starbuck."

"Let's say I've had to be," Jessie told him.

"Well . . . I guess you and Ki could help the most by being a sort of roving patrol," O'Connor went on thoughtfully. "Just ride around and make sure the fellows are on the job."

"You don't think some of them might feel that we're strangers who're mixing into something that's not really our affair?" Jessie asked.

"Oh, there's not much chance they'd feel put-on," O'Connor replied. "And things like this aren't exactly strange to some of them, but a few of them haven't been out here in the west long enough to understand how us old hands work."

Jessie nodded. "That's what we'll do, then. If you need us for anything special, just call."

She and Ki levered themselves into their saddles and started toward the road. For the first few minutes, until their body heat had dried out their saddles, they felt chilled in the raw flittering breezes that were gusting now. The gusts were coming faster, and the wind had freshened as the downpour continued. Big raindrops were swirling in the intermittent gusts, spattering on their slickers and landing with stinging force on the exposed skin of their faces and hands.

"I wish those outlaws had picked better weather for their robbery," Jessie told Ki as they approached the road. She nodded at the deep puddles that reflected the gray sky on their shimmering, rain-pocked surfaces. The puddles showed every few feet along the soaked trail—more a track now than a road—that closed the narrow V in which the canyon ended.

"There's one good thing about it," Ki replied. "If they should manage to give us the slip, they'd leave tracks that a two-year-old child could follow."

"With all the men that've come out from Medicine Lodge to join us, there's not much chance of the outlaws getting away," Jessie agreed. "And most of those men in the posse seem pretty sensible, the kind that think before they shoot."

"What surprises me is that the killers haven't tried to shoot their way out of that gulch," Ki went on. "Those two or three shots they let off when we first got here are the only ones they've fired."

"Maybe they're low on ammunition," Jessie suggested.

"Possibly," Ki nodded. "But from the way the inside of the bank looked, they didn't spare the shells then."

Jessie had been looking down the length of the canyon as they drew abreast of its narrow steep-walled end. She reined in, and Ki pulled his horse up beside her.

"What's wrong?" he asked.

"Nothing, Ki. I just noticed something for the first time, that's all."

"Noticed what?"

"Look down the canyon, doesn't there seem to be a lot more water on the canyon floor than there was when we first got here?"

"You're right," Ki agreed as he surveyed the canyon. "When we saw that gully for the first time it was just a tiny trickle. It's about three or four times as wide now as it was then."

"That's because the rain is pouring down the steep canyon slope," Jessie went on. "The water's rising, and forcing the gully to fill up. If it keeps raining hard, I'm sure the gully will get wider and deeper, maybe deep enough to fill the canyon completely."

As the implications of the natural phenomenon they were looking at sank into their minds, both Ki and Jessie smiled in spite of the serious reasons for their presence at the canyon. Ki took his eyes off the rising, yellowish water to look at Jessie and say, "Apparently nature doesn't have any more use for murderers than we do."

"Perhaps this time you're the one who's right, Ki," Jessie went on. "And it might be that all we'll have to do is wait for the rain to fill the canyon up some more. Those killers in the canyon will be forced to surrender when the water rises high enough to force them up this way."

"Or fight to break through our bunch if they want to get away," Ki suggested. His smile had disappeared now, and his face was sober.

"We wouldn't be here if we weren't ready to fight," Jessie reminded him. "And I'm sure that Barney O'Connor has noticed how the canyon's filling up."

"Maybe not. The brush is a lot higher and thicker back where he is. It'd hide the water level."

"Perhaps we'd better go back and tell him, then."

"There's no need for both of us to go," Ki suggested. "Why don't you go on, Jessie. I'll ride back and tell O'Connor."

"We do need to make sure that he sees what's going to happen in the next few hours." Jessie's voice was thoughtful.

"Of course he does," Ki agreed. "If he knows now, he can plan to have the men close to the rim to keep an eye on the water level in the gully and to move up this way as it gets deeper."

Jessie nodded. "Exactly what I was thinking, Ki. With the entire posse concentrated at this end of the canyon, the killers ought to be smart enough to see they're trapped. Maybe they'll give up without any more fighting."

"I'll go back and tell him, then," Ki offered. "You can warn the men on the other side of the canyon to keep an eye on the water level and move up this way as it gets deeper."

"Go ahead," Jessie nodded. "And I'll get the word to the others just as fast as I can."

Ki rode off and Jessie turned her horse. She held it on a short rein as it picked its way through the sheet of water that covered the surface of the cleft rock that formed the end of the canyon. The rain was still falling hard. Water was flowing fetlock-deep over the low elongated twin domes that marked the far end of the little canyon. Before Jessie could see bare earth ahead, her mount had shied twice as its ironshod hooves slid over the slick treacherous footing.

After taking what seemed a very long time to cover such a short distance, she reached the point where the slippery, solid rock gave way to the muddy morass which passed for earth. Jessie breathed a sigh of relief as she reached the soft yielding ground and let the animal have its head again.

Her progress was slow, for on this side of the draw the split in the great cleft granite formation was only a few yards from the point where it plunged downward. Thick undergrowth covered the ground to within a few yards of the granite, and Jessie's horse was forced to weave in and out of the dense dripping brush as it picked its way along the canyon rim.

Slow as her progress was over the mucky ground, Jessie saw another rider below in the canyon after she'd ridden for only a short distance. The man was a stranger to her.

"Hello, there!" she called. "I'm Jessica Starbuck, surrender and I'll see that—"

Then Jessie saw the stranger's hand dropping to the butt of his revolver.

In spite of her delay in recognizing that she'd made a

bad mistake, Jessie's draw was quicker than the outlaw's. Before he could draw and level his pistol, Jessie had her Colt in her hand. She triggered off a shot from the hip just as the livery horse lurched into a deep puddle, and its hooves slid in all directions while it struggled to keep from falling.

Jessie's slug missed, but the stranger's belated answering shot also cut empty air as he replied to her bullet. He was reining his horse into the thicker brush on the canyon floor before the animal Jessie rode had picked up its gait again.

Jessie held her fire rather than taking the risk of wasting a shot into the undergrowth that now made an uncertain target of the retreating outlaw. She scanned the brush, trying to get a clear look at the man. She could still hear his horse as it threshed its way through the dense high brush. All her eye-search was fruitless. Horse and rider alike were hidden by the thick cover of bushes that on this side of the canyon extended almost to the edge of the split.

After she'd pushed ahead a short distance, Jessie found that by bending forward in the saddle as far as possible she could get an occasional glimpse of the little canyon's rocky rim. She could still hear the outlaw churning through the bushes somewhere not too far below her.

Concentrating now on listening rather than looking, depending on her ears to guide her, Jessie kept moving while waiting for a clear view of the rider below. She did not holster her Colt, but kept it in her hand. She realized that in the heavy ground cover on this side of the canyon even her speed at drawing the weapon might not be enough for another clear shot.

• • •

Ki found O'Connor riding toward the mouth of the canyon and called to him. The posse leader reined in and waited for Ki to reach him.

"Did you and Miss Jessie run into trouble?" O'Connor asked.

"No. Jessie and I have had no problems. But both of us wondered if you'd noticed what's happening to the canyon."

"Can't say I have," O'Connor frowned. "Matter of fact, if you'll look down that way you'll find you can't see it too well because of the brush."

"That's what we were thinking," Ki said nodding. "Up by the road from town, where you can see down along the gully, you can tell that the water's flowing so deep and strong now that it's filling the canyon up. It's getting deeper every minute."

"Then that's going to force the killers to come up to the entrance of the canyon!" O'Connor exclaimed.

"Exactly," Ki nodded. "They're getting bottled up, pushed farther toward the sides."

"Which means they'll have to fight their way through us to get out, or they'll be drowned!"

"Suppose you promised them a fair trial if they gave up without fighting?" Ki suggested. "Maybe you could offer to take them to Wichita or even someplace else farther away to be tried?"

O'Connor shook his head. "They're not likely to believe me, even if I swore on a stack of Bibles that I'd do what I said."

"What if Jessie promised them a fair trial?"

"It'd be a toss-up if they'd believe her, or anybody else. No, Ki. When the water in the gully forces them up as far as the road, they'll have only two choices," O'Connor said, his voice hard. "Fight or give up."

"There's not much chance of the rain stopping." Ki gestured skyward where the rain clouds still hung, gray and heavy.

"We can't keep them from fighting to get out," O'Connor said. "They'll fight, because they know they've got to get away to save their skins. You can bet they know what's sure to happen once these Medicine Lodge folks get their hands on them."

"I take it you mean the people would lynch them?"

"There wouldn't be any way to stop them. Mr. Payne helped a lot of folks out, even before he bought the bank. Matter of fact, Ki, some of the smartest fellows in town say the only reason he bought out Blaise Caldwell was to be sure he didn't spend the bank broke."

"Caldwell was having money trouble, then?"

"All I've got to go by is the gossip I've heard, but everybody that knows Blaise tags him a real two-fisted spender. They say he spent about half his time over to Dodge City, bucking the big-money games the saloons have there."

"This is something that Jessie would be interested to hear."

"If she'd've got into town a little earlier and asked around, she'd've found out about him fast enough. Hell, I'll tell her myself when I see her. And why didn't she come with you, anyhow?"

"She's riding along the north rim of the canyon, telling the men watching that side to keep their eyes open. The killers will have to move up toward the road as the water rises."

"Which means I've got to get busy and warn the men on this side to do the same thing," O'Connor said. "And maybe you'd better be getting back to the road. Jessie might need some help if the killers move faster than you figured."

After her exchange of shots with the fugitive murderer, Jessie kept pushing ahead along the rim. She made slow progress through dense brush along the sides of the rain-swollen watercourse. The shrubs, saplings, and weeds seemed to grow even thicker as she advanced. She kept to the high ground and did not holster her Colt, but kept it in her hand.

Although she was in strange surroundings, Jessie could read the signs that nature had left along the littered canyon slope. Caught in the tangles of brush and shrubs that clung to the canyon's wall was older growth that had uprooted and washed up on other occasions. The dead vegetation, its bark peeling and its leaves gone, marked the high-water line of earlier floodings.

This line of deadwood told her that the water was already higher than its usual level. By watching the water's creeping edge, she could see its slow but steady rise, fed by the pelting rain that continued to fall. The rain continued without let up. Now and again it gusted into blindingly thick wind-tossed sheets, but even during the moments when the wind died the big drops kept pelting down from the lead-gray sky.

Urging the livery horse through an especially dense patch of wild growth, Jessie heard ahead of her the noise of someone else moving through the undergrowth. Taking no chances, she pulled her mount away from the edge of the slope into a grove of thick-leaved mulberry saplings. The baby trees did not hide her completely, but she sat calmly, Colt in her hand, and waited for the rider to reach a point where she could see him.

At first sight she did not recognize the man, but her instinct as well as the casual gait to which he was holding his horse hinted very strongly to her that he was one of the posse and not one of the fugitives.

"Over here, mister," she called to him as he approached, and as the rider swivelled in his saddle to look in her direction she added, "I don't remember your name, but—"

"John Fleming, Miss Starbuck," the rider said.

"Well, Mr. Fleming, I've got a message for you and the others who're watching this side of the canyon," Jessie went on. "Mr. O'Connor wants us to begin moving up toward the road. I guess you've noticed how fast the water's rising."

"I sure have," Fleming replied. "I was coming to find Barney and ask him if maybe we better get the whole posse bunched together and try to grab them killers when the water's high enough to make 'em push up to the road."

"If you'll ride back and tell the others what I've told you, I'll be greatly obliged," Jessie said. "The way things look now, all we're going to have to do is wait along the entrance and trap the killers when the water drives them far enough upstream."

"Sure. I'll be glad to," Fleming answered. "We'll just move slow and easy and keep our eyes peeled so none of them has a chance to git away."

"Good," Jessie nodded. "Just be sure that you stay behind the men in the canyon. They don't have a chance with the entire rim guarded. But don't shoot unless they shoot first."

"Don't worry about that," he said. "Me and the others got that all settled between us before we separated and strung out. There ain't a man jack of us that don't want to

61

see 'em git what they got coming to 'em, but we want it all legal and proper. A regular trial in front of a judge and jury, with a hangman's noose at the end of it."

With a wave to Jessie, Fleming turned his horse and started back along the rim. Jessie watched him ride out of sight, then wheeled her own mount and rode toward the road through the heavy rain that still showed no signs of letting up.

★

Chapter 6

"I'd say we've got about as tight a trap as anybody's ever put together," Ki observed.

"Our trap's all right, but I'd like to see those killers come up the gulch," Jessie replied.

They were sitting huddled in their saddles under one of the thick-leaved mulberry trees that formed a grove a few yards from the road. Beyond them the roily water still crept slowly up the canyon walls, but the heavy downpour that caused its sudden rise had ended a half-hour earlier.

Now, the drops came down only for short periods at a time. They were smaller and fell more gently, as April showers should. Though an occasional gust of the fickle wind still swept across the gully to sting their faces with a sudden spattering of tiny droplets, they could tell that the rainstorm had just about run its course.

"We've been out here along the road in this freezing rain for nearly two hours now," Jessie went on. There was no

63

note of complaint in her voice when she mentioned their long wait. She went on, "Once this trap's sprung, we can go back to Medicine Lodge and dry off and get warm."

"We could go back now if you want to, Jessie," Ki suggested. "There are more than enough men along the entrance here to handle four outlaws."

"I'd rather stay, Ki. We're really not all that uncomfortable, and we know the rising water's going to force that bunch up here sooner or later."

"When they do get here, there's almost certain to be a fight," Ki reminded her. "I don't imagine that they'll give up easily."

"They probably won't. But I have a very good reason for staying. The men from Medicine Lodge are about as angry as it's possible for humans to get. If we're here we might be able to get them to listen to reason and not string up the outlaws on one of these trees."

"You want to see the killers stand trial," he nodded.

"A court trial and legal execution would do a lot more to discourage other outlaws than a lynching party, Ki."

"Yes, you're right about that."

"And there's another reason," Jessie went on. "I suppose you could call it selfish, but word of a public trial would travel quite a way, and would probably attract Blaise Caldwell back here. He's the one I'm anxious to see."

"You've thought of everything, as usual," Ki smiled. "But the cold hard fact is that these men along the entrance aren't thinking about Caldwell. They want the men who shot the bank president and the bank teller."

"And so do I, of course. But—"

Jessie broke off as shouts arose downhill, along the canyon opening. She and Ki did not need to discuss what their course of action should be, but toed their horses into

64

motion and started for the area where the calls were loudest.

They did not have far to go. Their horses plodded downhill through the brush for one or two minutes. Their progress was slowed by thick soft mud, then they reached a spot on the incline overlooking the canyon entrance. Below, several men of the posse had gathered. The place where they reined in rose a dozen feet above the brush-lined gully.

They could see that the water at the bottom of the gully was now high enough to creep above a horse's fetlock. Above one of the thickest patches of brush and weeds that were strung along the banks of the watercourse, a long branch torn from a tree rose above the undergrowth. At the top of the branch a strip of white cloth fluttered in the cold fitful wind that blew off the water and rippled up the canyon.

"That's supposed to be a white flag, I guess," Jessie said to Ki as they reined in. "I hope it means the killers have finally decided to surrender."

John Fleming and another man unknown to Jessie and Ki had reined up in time to hear Jessie's remark.

"I hate to disappoint you, Miss Starbuck," Fleming said. "Nate here saw that white cloth just a few minutes ago and yelled for the rest of us to come along to where he was."

Jessie turned to the man called Nate and asked, "You didn't see anybody, I suppose?"

"Not a soul," he said, shaking his head. "I was riding back and forth along the bank here when I spotted the flag, but I didn't see anybody put the white flag up."

"And there's not any sign of the killers," Fleming added. "Just the flag."

"But surely they're somewhere close," Jessie frowned. "The flag didn't just get there by itself."

"No, of course not," Fleming agreed. "But we've been straining our eyes trying to see through those bushes ever since we got here, and we haven't seen anybody stirring in the gully yet."

His words might have been a cue for the unseen man whose voice came suddenly from one of the stands of brush. Fleming reacted with the quick instinctive move of one whose nerves were strained to the utmost. He brought up his rifle-muzzle and sent a shot into the brush in the general area from which the voice had come. Before he could trigger off a second shot a voice came from somewhere in the thick growth.

"Don't start shooting!" the unseen man called. "All we want is to parley! We're ready to make a deal with you."

"Like hell we'll make a deal!" Fleming shouted in response. "You know you can't get away! We're ready to wait till you get drowned out and have to give up!"

"If you want us that bad, come in and get us!" the man in the brush answered.

"We don't have to!" Fleming reminded the outlaw. "All we've got to do is wait. We've got all the time in the world, but you ain't that lucky."

"We've already palavered about what to do," the unseen killer replied. "We'll take our chances shooting our way out before we give up!"

"You're dead men any way you go!" Fleming shouted. He fell silent then, awaiting a response, but none came. Turning to the others he went on, "I guess he's gone."

"Well, you was real quick on the trigger with that blind shot you let off," Nate pointed out. "And you got pretty strong about them not having no place to git away to."

"Not as strong as I feel about 'em!" Fleming retorted. "I was good friends with Mr. Payne and George. I'm sorry I missed whoever it was down there, but I guess it was a fool shot, at that. Now, don't you expect to get me to back down, Nate! I mean to see those killers swing!"

"We're not going to get anywhere arguing," Jessie broke in quickly. "As far as I can see, the water's still rising in that gully. All we need to do is keep on being patient."

She did not go on. Hoofbeats, soft and muffled on the rain-soaked soil, reached their ears, and all four of them turned to see who was approaching. They saw Barney O'Connor, holding back on the reins of his horse as the animal floundered through the slick mucky soil on his way down the incline to the gully.

"Who'd you shoot?" he asked as he reined in.

"Nobody," Fleming replied sourly. "It was just a wild shot, and you can blame it on me. I guess I was out of line, but one of those murdering bastards yelled at us from down there in the bushes and it made me real mad."

"I don't guess you hit him?"

Fleming shook his head. "Not likely. I just shot blind."

"What was he yelling about?" O'Connor frowned.

"He wanted to make some kind of deal with us."

"And you haven't heard from him since?"

"Not a peep," Fleming answered.

"You're not even figuring to go look and see whether or not you did hit him?" O'Connor asked. "He might be down in that mess of weeds, and us not even know it."

"Hadn't even occurred to me that I ought to look," Fleming said. He glanced at the surface of the mud-brown water that was now lapping up the slope of the canyon entrance just below them and added, "But I guess I better, at that."

Dismounting, Fleming unbuckled his gun belt and draped it over his saddle horn. He drew the revolver from the belt's holster and tucked it into the waistband of his Levis, then began levering out of his boots.

"This is a new pair of Lucchese's best," he volunteered as he set one boot aside and started easing off the other, "or I wouldn't bother. But if I didn't take 'em off now, I'd have to take 'em off and empty 'em when I get back."

"You'll need a wading-staff," Ki said. "The bottom might be slick. You'll be all right if you just get your legs wet, but you might slip and fall in and get wet all over."

Looking at the trees that dotted the level ground beyond the incline, Ki finally found one with a broken drooping branch. Going to the tree, he wrenched the broken branch free and stripped it of its dead twigs. He returned to the others and handed the branch to Fleming, who nodded his thanks before he started down the embankment.

At the creek's edge, Fleming hesitated for a moment, then stepped into the murky roiled water. While the others watched from the incline, he picked his way carefully to the strip of flag and then beyond it to the brushy area where the outlaw had been hiding. The watchers on the incline saw him moving back and forth over a small area for several minutes, prodding with his improvised wading-staff among the bushes that rose above the surface. Then he turned and started back to the shore.

As he came within easy speaking distance of the bank Fleming said sourly, "Well, I guess you saw what I found. Just what the little boy shot at, nothing."

"Maybe you didn't find anything, but you showed us something that ought to make us feel better," Jessie told him. "We know now that those killers are being pushed."

"They've just about figured out that they'll be sitting

ducks for us as the water keeps getting deeper," O'Connor added. He swung out of his saddle and went down to the water's edge to give Fleming a hand getting up the incline.

"It's still coming up," Fleming said. He scraped his cupped palms along his legs and feet to rid them of the mud that he'd brought to shore from the gully bottom. "Another hour and it's going to be deep enough to wash against a horse's belly."

"We won't have to wait very long for the outlaws to make up their minds, then," Jessie told her companions. "When the top of the water gets to their stirrups, they'll either have to swim or start back up this way." She turned to O'Connor and added, "I'm not trying to give you any orders, but I've got a suggestion that might help us."

"Go ahead, Miss Starbuck," he invited.

"Let's start moving into the canyon along the sides of the gully. The killers are going to have to move pretty soon, and when they see how badly they're outnumbered, they'll realize that they only have two choices. They'll either have to give up or start a fight they'd be sure to lose."

For a moment O'Connor said nothing. Then he nodded and replied, "It's worth a try. We can ride slow and keep our eyes peeled so they don't have a chance to get the drop on us."

Jessie went on, "If we can get the drop on them and just hold them where they are, there's an outside chance they'd give up as the water keeps rising."

"You know, Miss Starbuck, the more I think about your idea the better I like it," O'Connor went on. He turned to one of the men and said, "Vern, how about you riding to the road. Tell the men up there what we're figuring to do, so they can be ready to go into the canyon with us. We'll ride slow and keep our eyes peeled. I've got a hunch Miss Starbuck's scheme just might work."

A few minutes of confusion followed before everyone in the group was mounted. They started along the gully bank, riding slowly toward the far end. Soon they saw the other members of the posse riding parallel along the opposite bank, but as they got closer to the end the ground began its downward slant and the little gully widened rapidly. The surface of the still-rising water was dotted with large patches of brush and clumps of trees with low-hanging branches that dipped down to meet the surface.

"This looks more like a lake now than a gully," Jessie remarked to Ki. "And there's certainly a lot more places where the outlaws can hide."

"In those stands of trees, for instance," Ki nodded. "Any one of them is big enough to shelter a half-dozen men."

In the area they'd reached now the water stretched for almost a mile from bank to bank. Jessie had been watching the dozens of tree-clusters ahead of them. They grew in stands or groves of six, eight, or ten, most of the clusters spaced widely apart. The tops of the trees stood high above the yellow water, but their lower branches dipped down to touch its roiling surface.

"I'm sure they've seen that for themselves, Ki," Jessie nodded. "And if they've had sense enough to scatter out and take cover where the trees are clumped, it'd be easy for them to catch us in a crossfire here and wipe us out before we figured where they're hiding."

"I don't like this at all," Ki agreed. His eyes caught the glimpse of a rider coming along the edge of the huge flood-pond from the direction of the canyon entrance. He pointed out the horseman to Jessie and went on, "That looks like Barney O'Connor. I'll bet he's seen the same thing we've just been talking about."

"It looks like we've run into something we didn't think about when we were talking," O'Connor called as soon as he was within easy speaking distance. "For all we know, the outlaws are hiding in those tree-clumps."

"Ki and I were just saying the same thing," Jessie replied. "Looking at what's ahead of us, I don't think my idea was such a good one. In fact, I'm beginning to wonder if it's wise for us to try to go any farther."

"I don't think it is," O'Connor told her. "But the outlaws are still in the same fix, maybe an even worse one."

"Yes, I've already seen that," Jessie replied. "They have to come out of wherever they're hiding and expose themselves if they're going to try making a getaway."

"Of course," he answered. "And I'm sure they've thought of the same thing."

"But do you think they'll do it?" Ki asked. "If I was in their position, I'd hold out as long as I could and see if the water goes down."

"Waiting's not going to help them," O'Connor pointed out. "Even if the water goes down, the ground's going to be too soft and slippery for their horses to move faster than a walk. They'll know that as well as we do."

"What, then?" Jessie asked.

"I'm thinking of trying to get them to surrender," O'Connor frowned. "Promise them that we won't lynch them. Guarantee that they'll have a fair trial instead of a vigilante lynching."

"Don't you think they're in too deep for something like that to have any effect?" Jessie asked.

"Well, all we can do is try, Miss Starbuck. Even if they don't take what they're offered, nothing will be changed."

"I'd try it, then," Jessie advised. "We certainly haven't anything to lose. We'll still have the upper hand."

"Here goes, then," O'Connor said. "I'll ride out where they can see me and try talking to them."

"You'd better carry a flag of truce of some kind," Jessie suggested. She took her handkerchief, white with an edge of lace, and passed it over to O'Connor. "Tie this on your rifle barrel and wave it now and then."

O'Connor took the hankerchief and looked at it thoughtfully for a moment, then said, "I guess I'd better tie it on a stick instead of my rifle, ma'am. It'd look a lot better."

"You're right," Jessie agreed. She looked around and saw a short length of broken branch. Her fingers moving nimbly, she tied a corner of the hankerchief to the tip of the branch and handed it to O'Connor. "Here. This ought to do the job," she said.

Waving the hankerchief, O'Connor rode down the slope to the edge of the flooded gully. After a moment of skittish dancing, his horse took to the water. The animal moved slowly, feeling its way with each hesitating step, until it got to a point midway between the stands of trees and the shore.

"That's close enough!" a man's voice sounded from one of the tree-clumps. "I got my sights on you, so don't try nothing funny! I guess we know what's on your mind, but spit it out anyhow!"

O'Connor had reined in at the speaker's first words. He called back, "All I want to do is offer you men a chance to surrender peacefully!"

"We've done figured out that's what you'd be saying," the fugitive's spokesman replied. "What's your offer?"

"Surrender and stand trial," O'Connor answered promptly.

"Hell, that don't get us nothing!" came the voice from the trees. "We want to go free!"

"I guess you do!" O'Connor retorted. "But there's one murdered man and another dying one you fellows have got to answer for. Now, you've got two choices. Give up, or we'll come after you!"

"Any time you feel like starting! We got plenty of shells, and the minute you-all hit the water we'll start using 'em!"

"There's four of you in there and fourteen of us out here!" O'Connor called. "What sort of chance do you think you'd have?"

"About as much as we would if we give up. Don't forget, you'll be sitting targets and shooting blind! We'll be hid, and we'll be aiming!"

On the shore, watching and listening, Ki said in a half-whisper to Jessie, "If all of them are like that fellow who's talking, O'Connor's not going to get very far."

"I really didn't expect him to, Ki," she answered. "Those men in the trees hold all the aces right now. All we can do is shoot blind, but they can drop down in the water behind their horses and shoot at us with very little risk."

"What do you think, then?" he asked.

"That if we want to take them alive, without any of us getting hurt or maybe killed, we'll have to wait."

"How long, Jessie?"

"Maybe until the water goes down. Maybe until they decide to break cover and try to get away. And don't forget, they've managed to get off scot-free so far. Not only that, they've got a lot more to lose by giving up than they have to gain."

73

Ki looked at the sky. "We've been so busy that I haven't paid much attention to the time," he told Jessie. "I can't quite believe that it's only about noon."

"We didn't have very far to ride," Jessie pointed out. "It didn't take us long to get our patrol along the gully set up. And there's no sun to remind us--" She broke off as O'Connor's voice sounded again from the gully.

"You men better change your minds while you've still got the time to!" he shouted. "I'll give you ten minutes to make up your minds, then we'll start shooting!"

"Ten minutes ain't enough!" the fugitive called back. "And if you start shooting, we'll match you bullet for bullet!"

"How much time do you want?" O'Connor asked.

"Give us a half-hour! We got a lot more to talk over than you have!"

O'Connor was silent for a moment, then he replied, "All right! You've got a half-hour. But when it's up, you'd better be ready to say yes or no. Remember, if you say no, that's when we'll start shooting!"

★

Chapter 7

As O'Connor reined his horse around and started back toward the shore, Jessie turned to Ki and said, "I'm not sure he did the right thing when he gave the killers more time. It's perfectly obvious what they're thinking."

"That the gully will drop and give them a chance to make a getaway?" he asked. "That occurred to me, but it's hopeless to expect that to happen, Jessie."

"Of course it is, Ki, but you've got to remember that here in Kansas a rain like this one isn't seen very often."

Ki glanced at the sky. It was still gray, and it promised more rainfall at any moment. He said, "Even if it doesn't rain another drop, this water's not going down more than a few inches during the rest of the day."

"You and I know that," Jessie told him. "But this might be the first time that people in this part of the country have seen these gullys and canyons flooded. We certainly haven't seen any signs of heavy rains anywhere near here."

"Then you figure the killers were just stalling for time, hoping they'd find some kind of chance to get away?"

"This is such a strange situation that I don't quite know what to say, Ki," she frowned. "Here we are in open country that's not really as open as it might be, with even the little gullys flooding. We've got a bunch of murderers pinned down, but they're not really pinned down tightly enough to be sure they can't slip away. And . . . well, you see what I'm getting at."

"Yes, I do," Ki nodded. "And we're also in a place that's strange to us, riding with a posse of greenhorns who're not quite sure of each other . . . or even of themselves."

"They're farmers, Ki, not cattlemen," Jessie said. "They don't have the same problems we do farther west."

"I suppose you're right," Ki agreed. He shrugged fatalistically and added, "I guess anything can happen from here on."

"I'm afraid you're right," Jessie agreed. "Now, if we were at home on the Circle Star or even a little bit farther west, where the real cattle country begins, I'd be able to judge things better."

"I'd say that O'Connor's already done the judging for us," Ki observed. "But he's almost here now. Maybe we can find out what sort of plan he's got in mind."

O'Connor splashed through the final few feet of shallow water and reined in as soon as his horse was on dry ground. He swung out of the saddle and faced the men of the posse, who'd been standing a short distance from the water's edge, watching during his parley with the killers. Jessie and Ki edged closer to the group.

"I guess everybody heard what we were saying back and forth out there," O'Connor said.

"We heard, all right," Taliaferro said. His voice was edgy and tight. "And there's some of us that think giving that bunch of killers more time wasn't the right thing to do."

"But there's some of us that don't think thataway," John Fleming said quickly. "A half-hour or so won't make all that much difference. This water won't start going down till late tonight, maybe not then. So even after the half-hour you gave 'em is past, we'll still have the murdering bastards pinned down."

"And with a mighty slim pin, if you can even call it that," Taliaferro put in. "I'd say we just got 'em by the skin of their teeth. No, sir! The only thing that's going to satisfy me is to see 'em on shore here, in handcuffs!"

"We'll get 'em here, all right," O'Connor said placatingly as he turned to face Taliaferro. "They don't have any place to go now, and from the way that one I talked to acted, I'd swear they know it. But let's give 'em the half-hour, Charley. It's still a long time until dark. In the meantime, you and George Friedley can go get reinforcements."

"I suppose you're right about that," Taliaferro replied grudgingly. "But at one minute past that half-hour you gave 'em, I say we better be ready to start shooting!"

Shutting his eyes to tiny slits, Ki glanced up at the sun. He then turned to Jessie. "O'Connor's half-hour's just about up, and the water's just as high as it ever was," he said.

"Maybe even a little bit higher," Jessie agreed. "If those killers expected it to drop so they could ride away, they've been badly disappointed. Now let's see what they do."

As though Ki's remark had been a cue, and even before Jessie could reply, one of the outlaws called from the

77

shelter of the grove of inundated trees. He did not show himself but remained hidden by the foliage.

"Hey, you on the bank!" he shouted. "Me and my boys has made up our minds. We got a sorta notion to give up. But you're going to hafta do what we want, or we won't make no kinda deal a'tall! We'll shoot it out!"

All of the men in the posse were now moving toward the water's edge. As she and Ki followed them, Jessie noticed that all of them carried their rifles. From the expressions on their faces most of them were prepared to start shooting.

Barney O'Connor pushed to the front of the group as the men walked toward the river. He cradled his rifle in the crook of his elbow and looked over his shoulder to be sure the entire party was behind him before replying to the fugitives.

"All right, we'll listen," O'Connor called through cupped hands. "What've you got to say?"

"We talked it out," the killers' spokesman replied. "And we're ready to give in."

"Then start toward shore and hold your guns up over your heads while you're coming in!" O'Connor commanded.

"Not so fast, mister!" the outlaw replied. "We don't trust you any more'n you trust us!"

"Stop beating around the bush and come right out with whatever you got on your mind, then!" O'Connor told the outlaw.

"We want protection!" the other man called. "I guess most of you's got a rope on your saddle. There's a lot of trees around here and we don't aim to decorate any of 'em!"

"What kind of protection do you expect?" O'Connor asked.

"We know right to a tee how many men you got with you," the unseen fugitive replied. "We been counting ever since you got here. Now, what we want is for every damned one of you to get down to the edge of this puddle where we can watch you while we're coming into shore. And we want to see you put all your guns on the ground before we even break our cover!"

"And how do we know you won't come out shooting?" O'Connor asked after a long, thoughtful pause.

"You don't," the fugitive retorted "But if we aimed to cut you down, we've had all the chance we needed while you fellows was parading up and down and acting like a bunch of chickens with their heads cut off!"

Jessie had been listening to the parleying between O'Connor and the killers. Now she lowered her voice and said to Ki, "We certainly aren't going to get anywhere as long as they keep on arguing this way. There must be somebody both of them will trust and listen to."

Ki shook his head. "I'm afraid not, Jessie. What we need is somebody like your father, who could—"

"That might be our answer, Ki!" Jessie broke in. "There aren't many people in the United States who haven't heard Alex Starbuck's name or have forgotten his reputation for strict honesty!"

"But Alex is—"

"I know," Jessie nodded. "But my name's Starbuck, too."

"As if I'd forgotten!" Ki retorted. He stopped short, frowning thoughtfully, then said, "But you're right. It might solve the problem. Are you sure you want to try? You'll be in a really exposed position, a clear target."

"Oh, I intend to try, Ki! If they accept my word, it'll put an end to the shooting and bring those men in peacefully."

"Then let's don't waste any time," Ki told her.

Jessie carried her rifle with her. Now she laid it aside, but she did not unbuckle and discard her gun belt. With Ki following her, she left the group of men and walked up to Barney O'Connor.

"Do you mind if I try to settle this?" she asked.

"You, Miss Starbuck?" O'Connor's jaw dropped and he stared at Jessie as though she was a visitor from another world. "How in—how do you think you can do that?"

"Please don't waste time!" she said. "Just ask those men out there if they've ever heard of Alex Starbuck. If even one of them says yes, tell them to listen to me."

His face showed his puzzlement, but O'Connor finally nodded his agreement. He turned back toward the copse where the killers were concealed and called, "Have any of you men out there ever heard the name Alex Starbuck?"

For a moment there was no reply, then the familiar voice of the outlaw who'd been speaking for the fugitives replied.

"I never did," he said. "But there's somebody here that has. Now, maybe you better tell us what that's got to do with anything?"

"Tell them who I am," Jessie urged O'Connor. "Ask them to listen to me for just one minute."

Turning back to face the outlaws' refuge, O'Connor shouted, "This lady standing by me here is Alex Starbuck's daughter. She's got something to say to you."

Jessie stepped as close to the water's edge as possible and called, "Which one of you men knew my father?"

There was a long moment of silence from the outlaws' hiding place. Then a strange voice replied, "I did, ma'am.

I handed for him down in south Texas when he was getting a herd together for that big ranch of his. The Circle Star, he called it."

"My name's Jessie. Think back, now. Did you ever hear my father speak of me?"

"Why, sure!" The unseen outlaw's reply came promptly. He went on, "You never was there while I was one of your daddy's hands, but I don't imagine any of us old boys missed hearing him brag about you."

"Did you ever hear of my father lying to anybody, or breaking his word?"

"No, ma'am, I sure didn't! Why, he was the straightest man I ever knew or even heard about!"

"Do you think I could be Alex Starbuck's daughter and lie to you?" Jessie called.

There was a pause, then the invisible speaker answered, "No, ma'am. Not if you're like your daddy was."

"Will you believe that I am like him?" Jessie pressed.

Again there was a pause before the answer came. "I . . . well, ma'am, I guess it's sorta reasonable to figure you are."

"Then listen to me!" Jessie said earnestly. "I'll guarantee that you and the men with you won't be shot by anybody who's standing here with me."

This time the silence that followed Jessie's words was longer than the earlier pauses. At last it was broken by the familiar voice of the fugitives' leader.

"Miss Starbuck," he called. "We know we ain't got much to trade with. There's two or three of you to every one of us. But if you'll take charge of the guns them fellers you're with has got, we'll come out peaceful and give up."

"You realize that all four of you will have to go to jail

81

and stand trial for shooting those two men at the bank, don't you?" Jessie asked.

Another pause followed, then the leader replied, "Sure we do. We've talked that all out. But we'd liefer do that than be shot down like a bunch of mangy dogs."

"I'll guarantee that won't happen to you. And I'll take charge of the rifles these men have," she said. "You can watch what we're doing over here. But you're going to have to hold your own rifles over your head with one hand while you're riding toward us. Just remember, I'm taking your word that you'll keep your side of our agreement."

"You got a deal, then, ma'am," the fugitive said. "Soon as we see them rifles stacked up, we'll come out. And we'll do like you said and hold our rifles over our heads."

"Are you crazy, Miss Starbuck?" O'Connor asked Jessie in the silence that followed. "Those men are outlaws, killers! They can't be trusted to keep any promise they make!"

"Is it better to take the chance that they will or to keep this stalemate going forever?" Jessie asked him. Then she added quickly, "Don't worry about it right now, Mr. O'Connor. Ki will take charge of your rifles. I've got my Colt and I'm a pretty fair shot."

"But what if they don't do like they promised?" O'Connor asked. "We can't trust them, Miss Starbuck!"

"Maybe not," Jessie replied. "But remember, they'll be holding their rifles over their heads with one hand, and they'll be using their other hand to keep hold of their reins. If they should start shooting, it'll take them a little time to get those rifles in action. If I see one of them so much as move to bring his gun down, I'll shoot him. And I'll guarantee to hold the rest of them off long enough for you to pick up your rifles."

"And you can depend on Jessie being able to outshoot any of them!" Ki added.

"Me, I think Miss Jessie's got a real deal worked out," John Fleming volunteered. "When you come right down to it, she did a better job getting 'em tamed down than any of the rest of us has been able to."

"I guess I've got to give you that," O'Connor admitted. "And I don't suppose we'd get too bad hurt if they don't do like they promised. All right, Miss Starbuck. It's your deal. So you go ahead and tell those fellows we'll see they get across the gully safe and sound."

Turning back to the gully, Jessie cupped her hands to her mouth and called, "I'll guarantee there won't be any shooting, unless you men shoot first!"

"Now, that sounds like something!" the outlaw replied. He was silent for a moment, then went on, "We won't shoot unless you start something, but we want your guns out in plain sight on shore there where we can see 'em!"

"We've already agreed to put our rifles in plain sight, and that's what we'll be doing next," Jessie told him. "And I'll promise you there's not going to be anybody hiding in the bushes to take a shot at you. I'll stand right here at the water's edge and watch while you're riding in."

During the time Jessie was talking to the fugitives, the men of the posse had been trailing past her to deposit their rifles in front of Ki, who stood a few yards beyond her. She looked around to make sure that there were no more rifles in the hands of the men, then turned back to call the fugitives.

"Any time you're ready, you can start for shore here," she told the still invisible killers. "Remember, keep your rifles over your heads while you're crossing."

A minute that seemed like an eternity ticked away before the first of the fugitives came out. He had obeyed Jessie's order, his rifle was held in one hand high above his head, his other hand was on the reins of his horse. He kept the animal reined in, moving slowly as his three partners in murder left the treetops and fell into line behind him. Like their leader, they carried their rifles in one hand, above their heads.

When the first of the killers broke cover, the men along the water's edge began whispering. By the time the last of their quarry had left the sheltering branches, the whispers had become louder. Though Jessie did not take her eyes off the fugitives, now and then she could catch snatches of the posse's low-voiced conversation.

"Damned if I thought they'd really give up," one of the men said.

"If it'd been me out there, I ain't a damned bit sure I'd've folded my hand so easy," another commented.

"One thing you got to give Miss Jessie credit for, she had the right idea," a third speaker told his companions.

"Damn right," still another agreed. "Even if I don't quite believe what I'm looking at."

"Sure saved us a heap of trouble," someone commented.

"I tell you one thing," the next speaker said. "I wouldn't bet a blind man a plugged penny that them bastards is going to be alive tomorrow."

"You know any of 'em?" still another asked.

"Not ary one. Never seen 'em in Medicine Lodge that I can recall," his companion replied.

"We'll find out who they are soon enough when we take 'em into town and lock 'em up," one of the men said.

Jessie was only vaguely aware of what was being said behind her; she was giving her full attention to the outlaws.

They'd covered more than half the distance now, and their faces were clearly visible. All of them were sprouting three-to four-day beards. They wore the clothing common to the west, and they all sported mustaches.

Three of them could have been any age from twenty to thirty. The face of the fourth was wrinkled and seamed with patches of grey in the grizzle that covered his cheeks and chin. In varying degrees, their faces were somber and angry. They reached the water's edge and reined up.

"Throw your rifles on the bank," Jessie commanded before any of them could speak. "And then toss your pistols over, too."

Wordlessly and reluctantly, moving with caution, the four men obeyed her. When all their weapons had landed on the soft rain-soaked ground, Jessie spoke again.

"I guess all of you have names," she said.

For a long moment none of the prisoners spoke. But after they had exchanged questioning glances, one of them replied, "It don't make no never-mind what our names are."

"You might as well tell us now," Jessie replied sternly. "I'm sure we'll find out your names and where you came from when we search your pockets and go through your saddlebags."

"Ah, hell!" one of the men exclaimed. "I guess what she says is right. They'll find out soon enough." Turning back to face Jessie he went on, "I'm Henry Newton Brown."

"William Smith," the man standing next to Brown volunteered.

Now that their companions had broken the ice, the other two spoke readily.

"John Wesley," one of them said.

"Ben Wheeler," the fourth announced. His voice was both angry and defiant.

"You're sure that's your right name?" Jessie frowned.

"I'm sure enough. If you don't like it, that ain't going to hurt my feelings none."

"Any name you claim is good enough for us if it's good enough for you," O'Connor broke in. "Now, the next thing we want to know is where you're from."

"Well, hell!" Brown blurted. "You got our names, so it wouldn't be hard to find out where we come from. Caldwell. It's east from here, down close to Indian Territory."

"You saved us quite a mite of trouble," O'Connor nodded. "We'd've found out sooner or later. All of you got kinfolks down there in Caldwell, I guess?"

Two nodded yes. But the one called Smith said, "Me and John hail from Texas."

"I guess the rest can wait," O'Connor told Jessie. "You sure done what you set out to, Miss Jessie."

"I try to finish any job I take on," Jessie replied. "But let's save any more questions until later. We'd better get them into town and locked up in jail."

"Well, now," O'Connor frowned. "One thing we sure haven't got in Medicine Lodge is a real jail."

"They're in your hands, then," Jessie nodded. "And Ki and I can get on with the business we came here to take care of."

"Hold on, now!" Brown protested. "Just wait a minute! You been lying to us all along, ain't you? You promised we'd get a fair trial, and now you're getting ready to string us up!"

"No!" Jessie said sharply. "You'll get the trial you were promised. All we're talking about is keeping you safe until we can get a judge and jury together." Turning to O'Connor she went on, "Surely there's somewhere in Medicine Lodge where these men can be locked up!"

"Oh, we've got a place Sam Denn uses for his lockup," O'Connor told her. "It's stout enough to hold 'em till we can take 'em to Wichita, where there's a real jail."

"That's the thing to do, then," Jessie nodded. "And there isn't any reason for us to stay here in this cold wet place any longer. I suggest we start back to town."

★

Chapter 8

"I can't really believe it, Ki."

Jessie was gesturing at the sky as she spoke. The clouds still hung low and grey, but they were higher now and several shades brighter than they had been when the rain was falling. Above the road far behind the little cavalcade that was riding ahead of Jessie and Ki a huge blotch of brightness behind the clouds marked the location of the westering sun.

She and Ki had chosen to let the posse lead the way on their return to Medicine Lodge. The volunteers had split into two groups, one riding ahead of the prisoners and the second behind them.

The captives' wrists had been tied to the saddlehorns of the horses they rode. The four killers sat their saddles uneasily with their shoulders slumped forward, their heads bowed, and their eyes fixed on the road.

Gesturing toward the huge half-glowing patch of sky

behind them, Jessie went on, "We've been so busy today that it seems like it should be getting dark by now, but from the location of the sun it's only a little past noon."

"It seems later than it is because we're not used to gray skies," Ki reminded her. "We're so accustomed to all the sunny days we get at the Circle Star that it's hard to keep track of the time in weather like this."

"At least the rain's stopped," Jessie said. "Now, if the clouds will just melt away, I'll be reasonably contented in spite of all the work that we still have to do."

"Compared to what we've been doing all morning, whatever's ahead ought to go by like a spring breeze."

"I'll probably feel better about everything when the messy job we've got to do first is finished."

"You mean the bank?"

Jessie nodded. "Yes."

"That sounds like you intend to take the authority of supervising the cleanup," Ki frowned.

"I've thought very hard about that, Ki." Jessie was frowning now, and her voice was sober. "It's all pretty badly mixed up. The one thing we're really sure of is that the loan Father made to Blaise Caldwell's father was secured by a mortgage on the bank and all its assets."

"So now with his father dead, Blaise Caldwell's responsible for paying you," Ki nodded.

"No, it's not all that simple," Jessie went on. "When Mr. Payne bought the bank from young Caldwell, I suppose he assumed the loan. That would make both the bank and Mr. Payne responsible for paying off the note.

"That's right," Jessie nodded. "So I'm going on the assumption that if Mr. Payne dies, it's the bank's responsibility to pay me. But the way things have happened in Medicine Lodge, and nobody knowing where Blaise Caldwell is, I'm pretty sure that I have the right to take charge of the bank and act as a temporary custodian until we can get it all straightened out."

Frowning now, Ki said, "I hope you're not going to try to open it for business, Jessie."

"Of course not. I might be on pretty shaky legal ground as it is, just moving in and taking charge without a court order appointing me an official custodian."

Ki said thoughtfully, "I don't suppose there's a judge closer than Wichita who'd have any jurisdiction in Medicine Lodge."

"No, I asked Barney O'Connor if there was. He said there's only one man in Medicine Lodge who has any official title, and that's Sam Denn, the town marshal. They had a justice of the peace, but he died about a month ago, and they haven't elected a new one yet to take his place."

"There really isn't anybody except Blaise Caldwell who'd be likely to give you any trouble if you took charge," Ki observed thoughtfully. "And nobody seems to know where he is."

"He's certainly dropped out of sight," Jessie agreed. "But if we do a little looking around and ask a few questions, I'm sure we can pick up his trail."

"Yes, it ought to be easy in a place as small as Medicine Lodge," Ki said. "But I'm beginning to wonder if he might have been smart enough not to leave a trail for us to follow."

"Oh, he must have! As soon as we get the bank in some sort of order, we'll start looking for him."

"What we have to do first is make sure that these murderers are put somewhere they can't get away from," Ki said.

"You don't think the building that Barney O'Connor told us about will hold them?" Jessie asked.

Ki shook his head. "Not from what Barney told me. It's what's left of a cabin-dugout on an old abandoned land-claim at the edge of town. Of course, the constable uses it as a jail, but it's probably not good for much except drunks."

"We'll certainly have to see that somebody stands guard over them, then."

"I'm sure O'Connor will think of that," Ki nodded. "If you want to, we can go look at the place to make sure."

"Yes. We'd better do that. And as soon as we've looked, I'm going to the hotel and have a hot sponge bath. Then I'll get into some dry clothes. I know I'm not wet and muddy all over, but right now I certainly feel like I am."

"That's a prescription I'll follow, too, Jessie. This Kansas wind certainly cuts into you when your clothes get wet."

"No worse than the Texas wind." Jessie smiled. "But not any better, either."

They could see the houses of Medicine Lodge now. After they'd ridden a short distance farther, O'Connor reined his horse off the road and led the posse across the open country to the edge of the little town. When the group was still a quarter-mile or more from Medicine Lodge's first houses, O'Connor brought the group to a halt in front of the weathered logs of what seemed to be only half a cabin. Its front wall was intact, it even had a board door that sagged from cracked leather hinges.

After Jessie and Ki had reined in, they saw that the cabin was one of a type that was once common on the Western frontier. Jessie and Ki had seen others exactly like it, especially in areas where building-sized logs were so scarce as to be almost nonexistent.

From the cabin's windowless front wall, the equally windowless sidewalls ran back into a low hillock. Enough dirt had been removed from the mound to create an enclosed interior. A backward slanting sheet-tin roof channelled rainwater beyond the high thick pile of dirt that formed half of the sides and the entire back of the cabin. Bracketing the hump of the soddie on each side were crescent-curved lines of long-dead trees, which rose above the mound made by the hybrid dwelling.

Even at first glance, it was obvious that the little soddie showed every possible sign of hard use, disuse, misuse and abandonment. However, Jessie realized as she inspected it that the structure was still solid. With a guard at the sagging door, there was no way by which the prisoners could escape without the long-time work of tunneling through the mound of earth at its rear.

"They should be safe enough in there," she told Ki. "But the door needs to be fixed up."

"Even the door's not mended it'll be easy for one guard to keep an eye on them," Ki agreed. "I think all that we need to do is talk to O'Connor for a minute or two, then we can go on to the hotel."

Nodding, Jessie said, "There's O'Connor, talking to Nate Priest and John Fleming. He must be asking them to take a shift as guards."

Dismounting, they walked the short distance to the three men. They got within earshot in time to hear O'Connor say, "If they try to get away, don't go soft-headed. Shoot to kill."

"Even if they haven't got guns?" Priest asked.

O'Connor countered with his own question. "Did

George Gephart and Mr. Payne have guns when these damn bastards shot 'em in the bank?"

"No. Or if they did, they didn't get a chance to use them," Priest said slowly.

"All right, Barney," Fleming put in. "We got the idea. There's four of them and two of us. We'll shoot, if they try to get away."

"I'll fix it up with some of the other boys to come take over after while," O'Connor went on. "We'll need to guard that bunch until we can fix up that door, or take 'em to Wichita or maybe even Hutchinson, wherever they'll be tried." He turned away from Priest and Fleming and saw Jessie and Ki. "Well," he said, "I guess we did what we set out to do. And we sure do appreciate the help you gave us, but I guess it's up to us men in Medicine Lodge now."

"Yes, it is," Jessie agreed. "And I see you've arranged for somebody to guard them."

"Oh, sure, Miss Starbuck," O'Connor nodded. "I don't want them to get away, that's for sure."

"And I suppose they'll get a fair trial?"

"They'll get a fair trial, all right," O'Connor replied. "But every man jack of us knows how it'll end. All four of them are going to wind up dancing at the end of a hangman's rope."

"I'm sure you're right," Jessie nodded. Then she went on, "Since you've got the situation in hand, there's no reason for us to stay. We'll be at the hotel if you should need us."

"I think me and the boys have got it all in hand, but thanks anyhow for offering," O'Connor told her.

Jessie acknowledged his thanks with a nod, then looked at Ki inquiringly. Ki read her silent message.

"Yes, let's go back to the hotel," he said.

"We've got one unpleasant job to do first," Jessie told him. "Arranging to get keys and the vault combination from a dying man, then giving our condolences to Gephart's people.

As they walked toward their horses he went on, "We'll both feel better after a hot bath and supper. And perhaps we won't have a long job tomorrow finding out what you need to know about the bank."

"I hope you're right, Ki," she replied. "At the moment I'm not too hopeful. This trip started well, but now it seems to have turned into something approaching a nightmare."

Alone in her room at the Medicine Lodge Hotel, Jessie took her time undressing while she waited for the hotel porter to fill the tub in the bathing room down the hall. When at last he tapped at the door and told her that the bath was ready, she hurried to it and lowered herself in the tin tub. A prolonged soaking washed from her mind the unpleasant moments of the last few hours.

She did not hurry her bath, but when the water began to cool she soaped and rinsed quickly. Then she slipped into her wrap and went back to her room. Letting the robe slide off her shoulders, Jessie blew out the kerosene lamp and gave a sigh of satisfaction as she stretched out on the bed. The last light pattering of raindrops from the dying storm whispered on the roof, making a tuneless, patternless lullaby. She closed her eyes, and after a few moments the recollections of the busy day faded. She began drifting into sleep.

She was very close to full slumber when the first distant shot broke the night's stillness. Jessie realized at once that the blast had come from a shotgun, it was a prolonged bass roar rather than the high-pitched crack of a rifle. There was total silence for a moment, then a scattered popping of pistol shots resounded from the distance.

Jessie had leaped out of bed when the shotgun spoke. After a moment's groping on the table beside the bed, she found matches and struck one to light the lamp. While she was lowering the chimney over the burning wick, the room still half-dark, a light tapping sounded from the door.

"Ki?" Jessie called, even though she was sure that he could be the only person in the hotel who'd be rapping.

"Yes," Ki replied. "I was sure you'd hear the shooting, or at least awakened by the sound."

"I was just on the edge of sleeping when I heard it start. I'll be dressed in a minute," Jessie told him. "But you know as well as I do what's happened."

As she spoke, Jessie was reaching for her clothes. She'd tossed her saddlebags aside after digging in them for a fresh outfit. Within a few moments after hearing the shooting, she was opening the door of her room to join Ki in the hall.

"It's a lynching-party at the soddie, of course," Jessie said as they hurried from the hotel.

"That's all it could be," Ki agreed. "And we'll save time by walking. Who knows where the liveryman is at this time of the evening."

"He may be out there now," Jessie replied. "And I suppose we ought've known this would happen. But I—" She stopped as two men rushed past them at a jog, talking loudly between gasps for breath as they ran.

"Damn it, I told you to hurry!" one of them was saying.

"Couldn't get ready no faster," his companion replied.

"You and your shuffling around!"

95

"Hell, we'll get there in time if you save your wind for running instead of talking!"

"I guess we should've foreseen this," Jessie said as the running men faded into the darkness ahead.

"It's not our fault. O'Connor told us they had all the men they needed," Ki said.

Faint shots were sounding now from the direction of the half-soddie where the outlaws had been confined. The hump that the building made in the flat, featureless Kansas prairie could be seen now. It was outlined by the bobbing lights of lanterns glowing yellow, which threw into distorted silhouettes the forms of the men milling around it.

Excited shouts suddenly rose from the crowd around the soddie. By now Jessie and Ki were more than halfway to the spot where the silhouettes of moving men showed against the glow of lantern-light. Suddenly, Jessie slowed their pace.

"Running won't help us now, Ki," she said. "We've both heard yells like that before, after a lynching."

"I'm afraid you're right," he agreed as he slowed his pace to match hers. "Do you want to go back to the hotel?"

"We're so close now that we might as well go on. After we left the outlaws may have said something that would be useful for us to know."

"It might be worth a try," Ki agreed. "After something like this happens in a little place like Medicine Lodge the town's always noisy and upset for the rest of the night."

Jessie and Ki had been scanning the scene while they talked. They needed no interpreters to tell them what had happened. From the branches of three of the dead trees that curved along the side of the soddie nearest them, the limp bodies of three men swayed at the ends of taut ropes in slow ghoulish circling movements. Though the darkness

and intermittent gleams of light made their features difficult to distinguish, there was no doubt of their identities.

Turning to Ki with a puzzled frown, Jessie said, "There
are only three of them here. Where could the other man
be?"

"Inside, maybe," he suggested. "He might've been shot
before the others were captured."

"I suppose it's possible," she said. "But when—"

"If you're looking for the other man," Barney O'Connor's voice behind them said, "he's laying out from the
soddie a ways, he was the one they killed first, from what
I've gathered."

Turning to face O'Connor, Jessie asked, "Then you
weren't here when the lynch mob arrived?"

"No, ma'am. Sam Denn was handlin' everything. I'd
gone into town to get some supper. I was in the middle of
eating when I heard some fellows in the cafe talking about
how it'd been planned. I left right away, but I was a mite
too late getting back."

"You mean that you didn't get here until all the prisoners were dead?" Ki frowned.

"They were just like they are now by the time I got
here," O'Connor answered. "That fellow who called his-
self Henry Newton Brown had already been shot and
killed, and the other three were swinging from the trees
there when I showed up."

"You don't have any idea who started the lynching?"
Jessie frowned.

O'Connor shook his head. "Not a notion."

Jessie went on, "But from what you've already told us,
all this had been planned."

"Oh, sure," O'Connor agreed. "You and Ki hadn't
hardly got started to town before there was men coming

out, and I'll tell you straight that they had this in mind. Friends of the men that got shot in the bank, I'd guess."

"Yes, I'm sure that's right," Jessie nodded. "They were both in very influential positions."

"Anyhow, I'd guess they were the ones that started the lynch-talk," O'Connor went on. "But I don't suppose it'd do anybody much good, even if we could say who they are."

"Not a bit," Jessie agreed. "The time to've stopped it was before they started moving."

"Oh, I think they had somebody out here who was on their side," O'Connor told her. "Maybe even some of the fellows who rode with us looking for the gang."

"I can't understand how that first man got shot," Ki said thoughtfully. "How did he get out of the soddie at all?"

"Well, right after you and Miss Jessie left, this Brown fellow said he wanted some paper and pencil to write his wife a note. We scrounged around and got him a couple of old envelopes and a pencil, then locked up again. He was still locked up when I left for supper."

"I'm afraid I don't follow you," Jessie frowned.

"Then Sam Denn opened the door to get Brown's letter and mail it," O'Connor explained. "He was overpowered by the crowd. Brown busted out running, and somebody pulled down on him with a shotgun. Just about cut him in two, it was such close range."

"I suppose the others came out then?" Jessie suggested.

"You're right as rain, Miss Starbuck," O'Connor nodded. "One of the outlaws that came out first got hit, but it didn't kill him. But it slowed down the outlaws, and the men around the soddie wrestled 'em down. By that time, somebody'd yelled they oughta be hung, so that's what they did. They went ahead and strung 'em up."

"There's certainly nothing we can do to turn the clock back, Ki," Jessie said after O'Connor had finished his story. "All the outlaws are dead."

Ki nodded and said, "Not the way things stand now. And as you mentioned earlier, it really isn't our affair. So I suggest that we go back to the hotel and get the sleep that we need so we'll be fresh for tomorrow."

Walking slowly, the effects of their long day and the sudden shock of the night's events beginning to show now, Jessie and Ki started back to Medicine Lodge.

★

Chapter 9

"You know, Ki, it's just occurred to me that we've been neglecting something," Jessie said as they walked through the darkness. Ahead of them the lights of Medicine Lodge no longer showed as a single luminous blur. They had separated now into individual widely-spaced dots.

"You must mean our stomachs," Ki replied.

"You're as hungry as I am, then?"

"I must be, Jessie. Maybe even more. We've been too busy today to pay much attention to eating."

"Or much of anything else. It's strange, but I was feeling very downcast when we got to the hotel after finishing that sad job we had to do. And I should've felt badly after seeing those outlaws the crowd killed. But . . . well, I feel like our job's almost finished here, and it's like a cloud's passed over, and in spite of the night, I feel a lot better."

"I'm glad," Ki nodded. "Now a little food should carry your blues away completely. The only question now is where are we going to find something to eat."

"Yes, Medicine Lodge is a farming town, not a cow-town where the restaurants and saloons stay open around the clock," Jessie said. "Do you think that either of the restaurants there will still be open at this time of night?"

"It's not all that late," Ki pointed out. "We just feel like it is."

"Let's walk faster, then. I've suddenly realized that I'm starving."

They stepped up their leisurely pace and watched the lights vanish as the houses of the town blocked their view. When they finally turned into the town's abbreviated main street, only two gleams of lamplight were visible. One was a nightlight shining through the glass-paned door of the hotel, and up the street beyond it a brighter glow came from the windows and open door of one of the little settlement's two cafes. Several horses stood at the hitch-rail in front of the restaurant.

"We're in luck," Jessie said. "But from the number of horses at the hitch-rail in front of it that restaurant's doing a lot of business tonight. Let's hope they've still got some food left in their kitchen."

As they got closer to the restaurant they could see that it was crowded. Picking their way across the rutted street, still wet and mushy from the day's rain, they could make out men lining the counter, filling every stool for the full length of the narrow rectangular interior.

Going up the steps, they saw that the half-dozen tables were also occupied. But as they went through the door, they spotted one table at the back of the room where a single patron sat and the remaining three chairs were vacant. The smell of food filled the air, whetting their appetites anew. They hurried to the open table.

"Would you mind sharing your table with us?" Jessie asked the lone diner. He was eating a steak, and when she looked at the large piece of meat that still remained on his platter, she suddenly realized how hungry she really was.

"Not a bit, ma'am," the man said. "But before you and your friend sit down, I better tell you. There's no waiter, so y'all will have to go to the kitchen to put in your order."

"Steak for you, Jessie?" Ki asked. "That's what I intend to have."

"Steak will be fine," Jessie replied. When Ki started for the kitchen, she took a chair at one side of the table's occupant. From a few unhappy experiences she'd learned that some people dining alone objected to close contact with Orientals, so she left the chair across from the table's occupant for Ki.

"Just don't mind if I'm not real good company," the man said apologetically, poising on his fork the bite of steak he'd just cut. "But I've been in the saddle all day without a meal, and I'm still too starved right now to talk a lot."

"Please don't feel obliged to talk with me," Jessie told him. "Ki and I have spent most of the day the same way you did."

Her companion was chewing the bite of meat he'd just cut and he acknowledged Jessie's remark with a nod. After he'd swallowed, he sank his fork into the steak and began cutting off another bite. While he was slicing it he asked, "Riding in from someplace, I guess?"

"No. Riding with the posse that went out to hunt down four killers and bring them in."

For a moment the man did not seem to grasp Jessie's level-voiced reply. He started to raise the fork to his mouth, then a frown rippled over his face. He held the bite of meat in mid-air as he asked, "Did I hear you right, ma'am? You went out with the posse that brought in those murdering rascals that was trying to rob the bank, the four that got lynched just a little while ago?"

Jessie nodded. "Yes, of course."

"Why, what those outlaws did and how they got what was coming to them is all I've heard about since I got off my horse!" he exclaimed. "If you don't mind my asking, how'd you get the posse to let a lady go along?"

"Ki and I rode into town just a few minutes after the holdup men had left. Our first stop was the bank; I had to go there to find out about some business matters that I was worried about."

"And how'd that get you a place in the posse?"

"When we heard what had happened, we talked the posse into letting us go along. But, please, don't let me take your attention off your supper. Go on and finish your meal before your steak gets cold."

"Now, that's real thoughtful of you, ma'am. But if you don't mind talking about it, I'd sure like to have you tell me whatall happened. I've heard so much gabbling about that posse since I got here, and most of the stories different, that I'm curious to know what really happened."

"There's not a great deal to tell," Jessie replied. "When Ki and I rode into town the robbers had already made their getaway. We stopped at the bank and found out what had happened. Then a young man named Barney O'Connor began gathering a posse. Ki and I were already saddled up, so we joined it."

By this time Jessie's table companion had chewed and swallowed his bite of meat. He said, "From the talk I've heard, they gave you quite a chase."

"It really wasn't all that much of one. We were lucky

and got on their trail right away. The rain had just started, but it hadn't come down hard enough to wash away their hoofprints. We saw where they'd turned off the road and the killers made the mistake of trying to hide in the gully of a canyon not far from town. When we located them, we kept them pinned down in the gully and just waited for the rising water to force them to come out and give up."

"Do I understand rightly that there wasn't any shooting?"

"Oh, a shot or two, but nobody was killed or even wounded. And I suppose you've heard all about what happened later, after we'd brought them back and put them into a soddie just outside town."

"You mean how they got killed?"

"Yes," Jessie nodded. "I can't say much about that, since Ki and I had come into town by then and weren't there. We went back to the soddie when the shooting started, but by the time we got there it was all over."

"Then it was the townfolks that wiped out the outlaws, not the posse?"

Before Jessie could answer, Ki returned carrying a large platter in each hand. He put one on the table at Jessie's place and the other in front of the empty chair opposite the stranger.

Jessie turned to their table companion and said, "We got started talking about the bank robbers before we had a chance to introduce ourselves."

"And it wasn't very polite of me to forget my manners," he nodded. "I'm Bob Hazen, in town here from Dodge City."

"And my name is Jessica Starbuck. This is Ki, who helps me run my ranch down in southwest Texas and keep track of my other business matters."

104

From the instant Jessie spoke her name, the stranger's eyes had begun bulging. As he nodded to acknowledge her introductions he said, "There can't be more than one Starbuck in this part of the country. That ranch you just mentioned has got to be the Circle Star, and you're bound to be Alex's daughter."

"Yes, I am," Jessie nodded. "And from what you just said you must've known my father."

"I sure did, a long time ago, when there weren't so many people in these parts. As a matter of fact, I helped him locate a man he hadn't been able to find who owned a lot of the land Alex needed to put the Circle Star together."

"Yes," Ki put in. "I remember him speaking of you, Mr. Hazen. But I didn't go to Texas with Alex on that trip, I stayed behind to keep an eye on some other pending business. Let's see . . . you were a stockman in Fort Worth at that time."

"That's right," Hazen agreed. "But I moved out of Texas a little while after I helped Alex with his deal. I'm located in Dodge City now. Got a cattle brokerage business there."

"I can't even begin to count the number of people I've met who remember Alex," Jessie said reflectively. "There's a man here in Medicine Lodge who met him years ago when they were both prospecting in the Yukon. He helped persuade the posse to let Ki and me go along to run down those killers."

"Anybody who ever knew Alex would sure help you, Miss Jessie," Hazen told her. "I know I sure would. When we first got to talking, you said that you came up here on some business connected with the Medicine Lodge Bank. Did Blaise Caldwell have anything to do with what you're here for?"

"You know him?" Jessie asked Hazen.

"Why, sure I do. But I knew his daddy better than I do Blaise. Kent Caldwell was a lot more man than that boy of his."

"Yes, Alex's business was always with Kent," Ki put in. "I met him a time or two when he was visiting with Alex."

"I do have some important business with Blaise Caldwell," Jessie said. "Now that the man who bought the bank from him is dying, I have to find out whether it will revert to Blaise, or what will happen to it."

"I gather from what you say that you've still got some money tied up in it?" Hazen asked.

"Alex helped Kent Caldwell to finance it," Jessie replied. "I had a letter from Blaise quite some time ago regarding paying me on a promissory note that's due. When I didn't hear from him again, I decided it might be wise to come here and take a look at the situation."

"I'd have to say that you made a good move," Hazen said slowly. "I suppose there's a pretty substantial sum involved?"

"Quite substantial," she nodded. "Of course, I don't know what the bank's situation is, and that might have an effect on Blaise being able to pay. I don't suppose you'd know where he is right now?"

Hazen shook his head. "He's a pretty regular visitor in Dodge, but I haven't run into him there lately. Right now I'm heading for the Texas Panhandle on a buying trip. I'll be going through Tascosa, and I know Blaise spends some time there."

Jessie frowned as she asked, "How can a bank in a small town like this handle business in Texas?"

"I don't imagine their business in Texas is such a much," Hazen told her. "Blaise goes down to the Panhandle for the high-stakes games in Tascosa. He's a real high-roller, from what he's let drop when we've been talking."

All three of them had continued eating while they talked, and by now their plates held only steak-bones. Jessie pushed her plate aside and stood up. Ki followed her example, and Hazen stood up a bit belatedly. While Ki stopped to settle their bill, Jessie and Hazen went out into the street.

"I'm long overdue for bed," Jessie said. "It's been a very long and very busy day."

"Then I'll bid you goodnight, Miss Starbuck," Hazen told her. "There's enough of an old cowhand left in me to enjoy sleeping under the stars, which is something I don't have much chance to do these days. But that's what I aim to do tonight. I'll just push on a ways before I spread my bedroll."

"You might have trouble finding a dry spot," Ki warned as he came out of the cafe. "The rain really came down today."

"Oh, I don't worry about that," Hazen smiled. "I know a dozen places up ahead where I can sleep, places I've bedded down in before there were any towns or railroads."

With a final wave, Hazen walked to his horse and mounted. Jessie and Ki turned and started back to the hotel. The night air was cool after the rain, and they walked briskly without talking until they reached their destination.

"We'll get an early start in the morning, Ki," Jessie said as they parted in the hotel hallway. "Things have been happening so fast since we got here that we really haven't had any time to plan ahead. We'd better get right to the most important job and see how much information we can get

107

from the bank ledgers. That's liable to take quite a lot of time."

"We're not going to be looking at the books of a big bank, Jessie," Ki reminded her. "We might find that we can get the job done in a day."

"It'll be nice if that's possible," Jessie agreed. "But small banks can have problems that're just as complicated as big ones. Anyhow, we'll see soon enough. Now I'm going to try for the second time tonight to get some sleep."

Early morning found Jessie and Ki hard at work in the bank. They'd started for the bank before Medicine Lodge was awake and stirring, and Jessie had taken the precaution of locking the door after they got inside and pulling the shades down on all the windows to forestall the peeping eyes of the curious.

Once inside, they'd begun by checking through the drawers of the desks used by the bank's two dead officers. These yielded little of any interest. They were filled with correspondence and a few personal items.

"But that's something we can understand," Jessie said after they'd completed their search. "Those two men had only been in charge of the bank for a few weeks. And I think we can be sure that Blaise Caldwell emptied the drawers before he turned things over to them."

"Then let's start going through the daily ledgers," Ki suggested. "They're probably kept in the vault."

Jessie used the combination she'd gotten from the dying Payne and opened the walk-in vault. One wall was filled with tiers of safety-deposit boxes, along the others there were shelves and cabinets laden with ledgers and boxed records.

"I'm sure there are master keys on this ring Payne's

wife gave me that will open everything in here," Jessie said, studying the keys in her hand. "It's just a matter of trial and error to find out which key fits in these locks."

"I'm sure I could open all of them with a little piece of wire," Ki smiled. "Picking intricate locks was part of my *ninjutsu* training."

"We'll get along just as well with the keys," Jessie told him. She handed him the keyring. "But it might be easier for you to do the unlocking."

"Shall we look at the cabinets first?" he suggested. "My guess is that the current ledgers are in one of them."

"Go ahead," Jessie said. "It sounds to me like you have the right idea."

Their search ended almost as soon as it had begun, for the daily master account ledgers were in the first cabinet Ki opened.

"You start from one end, I'll start from the other," Jessie suggested. "But remember that we're a lot more interested in the time when Blaise Caldwell owned the bank than we are with the short time Mr. Payne had it."

Selecting the ledgers bearing the latest dates on their spines was an easy matter. Carrying the two massive account books to the desks outside the vault, Ki put a ledger on each one.

"Take your choice," he said with a wave of his hand. "Past or current, whichever you prefer."

"I'll just sit down here at the desk I'm standing by," she replied. Settling into the desk chair, she glanced at the spine of the ledger she'd chosen. "You must have the new ledger that starts when Payne took over the bank. This one that I have covers Blaise Caldwell's last few years as owner after his father died and before he sold to Payne."

"That's right," Ki agreed after glancing at the first pages

of the ledger on the desk nearest him. "Now let's see what we can find out."

Both he and Jessie got busy at once, leafing through the pages of the ledgers they'd chosen. Jessie began her examination at the back pages of her ledger. She went through the thick lined pages filled with Caldwell's entries for almost a full hour before looking up at Ki.

"I don't know what you're finding," she told Ki. "But in this ledger I see a pattern that I certainly don't like."

"Embezzlement?" Ki frowned.

"I'm sure it is," she nodded. "And from our experiences with the occasional bad apple that's tried to defraud one of the Starbuck banks, Caldwell's stealing follows a pretty common pattern."

"I think I know what you mean," Ki nodded. "Blaise Caldwell kept just about enough cash on hand from the deposits made every day to cover the average withdrawals. Am I right?"

"Completely," Jessie agreed. "And put the surplus that he had into his own pocket."

"And I don't suppose there's anything in the entries that might give us a hint where he tucked away the money he stole?"

Jessie shook her head. "Of course not! But it must've been someplace handy, in case he didn't judge a day's cash turnover correctly. He'd have to be able to get his hands on the money he'd put aside to cover that kind of situation."

"A safety deposit box under some assumed name, right here in the bank," Ki suggested.

"Yes. That'd be his only protection. He'd have to be able to get his hands on the money quickly."

"Then do you think we need to look any further, now

that we're reasonably sure that's how he worked his thefts?"

"Keep on looking through the ledgers?" Jessie asked.

"No, looking through the safety deposit boxes. There must be a master key somewhere on the key ring."

"I'm sure there is," Jessie answered. "But I haven't run across yet anything that would give us a hint where all the surplus money went, other than Caldwell's pockets."

Ki shook his head. "No. He'd just withdraw the money on a personal cash memorandum. The money simply vanished."

"Now that we're pretty sure of the pattern Caldwell followed in his thefts, I don't think we need to look any further at the ledgers," Jessie suggested.

"I suppose you're right. Now we're going to have to open any suspicious safety deposit boxes and see if there's any money in them."

"Yes, I agree with you. There can't be too many, in a bank as small as this one. But both of us know what a job that can turn out to be," Jessie reminded him.

"Perhaps it isn't as bad as it seems. There's sure to be a list of safety deposit boxholders in one of those ledgers we found a few minutes ago."

"Yes, of course!" Jessie agreed. "And in one of those boxes we're likely to find the evidence we need to convict Caldwell."

"We'll have to find him first."

"I know," Jessie nodded. "And thanks to meeting Bob Hazen last night, we've got the clues we need to put us on Caldwell's trail. Let's begin looking, Ki! The sooner we catch up with that man, the better I'll like it!"

★

Chapter 10

"It's been a while since our last visit to Dodge City, Ki," Jessie remarked.

"I don't suppose it's changed much, though," Ki answered.

They were riding toward Dodge City with the setting sun in their eyes. Against the blinding glare of sunset that stretched from end to end of the level and otherwise featureless horizon, they were now getting their first glimpse of the town's houses and commercial buildings as black silhouettes.

Both were saddle-weary, for they'd spent two days pushing steadily west from Medicine Lodge after finishing their examination of the bank's affairs. The rest of their long day of checking the bank's vault and tills at the two cashiers' windows had revealed a surprisingly small amount of cash. There were a few substantial sums in individual safety deposit boxes, but the almost-bare main vault had confirmed Jessie's intuitive suspicion that the bank had been stripped of cash before its change of owners.

By checking through the ledgers Jessie and Ki had managed to identify the private safety deposit box belonging to Blaise Caldwell. Like all the others, it opened with one of the keys on Payne's key ring, but when opened it had been completely empty, not only of cash, but of even a shred of paper that might have given them a clue as to his whereabouts.

"I'm not going to let Caldwell get away with this!" Jessie had exclaimed angrily, staring at the empty box. "It's not just the damage he's done me by ruining the bank, Ki. I can stand the loss without being hurt, but there are a lot of good people here in Medicine Lodge who'd be ruined by losing whatever cash he's been able to steal from them!"

"We'll have to find him first," Ki had reminded her.

"Then we will! And we'll have to move fast, before he has time to lose every penny of it in the gambling joints."

They'd pushed their horses to the limit as they followed the now little-used cattle trails west. First they'd cut in a beeline across the level prairie between the Cimarron and Arkansas Rivers. The going had been easy, for the pounding hooves of many thousand steers during the years of trail-driving had left a broad swathe across the rolling terrain.

At last they'd splashed through the shallows of the Arkansas River's northeastern bend and picked up the old military road that led to Fort Dodge. The road was still in good condition from constant use, and they were now on the last leg of their journey. The houses of Dodge City loomed on the horizon, which was now beginning to turn pink with the sunset.

"We'll soon know what Dodge is like these days," Ki

told Jessie as the lines of the town's buildings grew more and more distinct. "It looks to me like it's grown quite a bit since the last time we were here."

"I wouldn't bet on that, Ki," Jessie frowned. "The way all the railroads have been pushing out branch lines, Dodge isn't the only place now where market herds can be loaded for shipping. The town's bound to've lost a lot of business."

"It's a tough place, Jessie. It wouldn't just fold up and die overnight. I'm sure there are still enough cattle being shipped from there to keep the town going."

"Do you suppose it's still as wild as ever?"

"Probably not quite," Ki replied thoughtfully. "But I'll bet we find out that it's living up to its reputation." Then he added as an afterthought, "Or trying to, at least."

"We'll find out soon enough," she said. "Another half-hour or so and we ought to be riding up Main Street. I guess the Dodge House is still the best place to stay."

"It always has been, since our first visit here. If Blaise Caldwell is still in town, that's probably where he's staying."

"Yes, confirmed gamblers like Caldwell can't afford to go second-class," Jessie nodded. "They'd lose their reputation if they did that."

They rode on in silence through Dodge City's scattered outskirts, then turned onto Main Street. Even at this early hour of the evening it was busy, though not yet crowded with the bustle that Jessie remembered. Most of the men on the street moved without haste. Half or more of them could be identified as trail hands, for they wore their denim working clothes and, here and there, some still sported chaps. The remainder were city-dwellers by their dress.

However, many of them shared one habit. They moved

often and stopped frequently to study the beckoning signs on the doors of all the gaming-houses, mulling over the lists of games of chance which were available inside, trying to decide which one to enter. Only a few moved with steady purpose, shouldering their way along the board sidewalks to the house of chance they'd already decided to let relieve them of their money.

"Dodge doesn't seem as crowded as it used to be, Ki," Jessie remarked as they rode slowly along the street.

"Perhaps not," Ki agreed. "But there are still enough people here to keep all the gambling palaces pretty busy."

"There's certainly been no change in that respect," she agreed. "Their business seems to be just about the same as always."

By this time they'd reached the Dodge House. Jessie led the way to the hotel's livery yard. After dismounting and taking their saddlebags off the animals, they left the liveryman to see to the horses and walked the few steps across the yard to the hotel. At that hour, the small cramped lobby was deserted except for the desk clerk.

"I'd like the same two bedroom suite that you provided the last time I stopped here," Jessie told the clerk after signing the register.

After glancing at her signature, the clerk replied with a nod that was half a bow, "Certainly, Miss Starbuck. And is there anything else that you require?"

"Perhaps you can help me with a bit of information," she answered. "I understand that Mr. Blaise Caldwell from Medicine Lodge also stops here when he's in town."

"Yes, indeed," the clerk replied. "He's one of our very regular patrons."

"Does he happen to be here now?" Jessie went on.

"Mr. Caldwell is indeed in residence," the clerk told

her. As Jessie and Ki exchanged glances, the man behind the desk went on, "But he's not in the hotel at the moment. I'll be glad to inform him of your inquiry, of course, and—"

"Oh, no!" Jessie broke in. "You see, I want to surprise him. In fact, I'll be very grateful if you'll say nothing whatever to Mr. Caldwell about my being here."

"Why, certainly," the clerk agreed. "And I'll tell the day clerk of your request as well, Miss Starbuck. You can be sure that we won't spoil your surprise."

"Thank you," Jessie nodded. She turned to Ki and went on, "I think I'd like to have dinner in our rooms, Ki. Does that fit in with your plans?"

"I haven't really made any plans," Ki replied. "But if you don't mind eating alone, this might be a good time for me to take a look along Main Street."

"Looking for someone in particular, I'm sure," Jessie smiled.

"Of course. I don't suppose I'll be lucky enough to run into him. But if I might find him somewhere away from the hotel, it could save us a lot of time and trouble."

"In that case, I certainly don't mind eating alone," Jessie said. "I hope you have good luck during your stroll."

"So do I. And I shouldn't be gone long. Dodge City isn't all that big, an hour at the most."

Ki took his time as he began his walk along Main Street. He was careful to give the appearance of a new arrival in town who'd set out to study the attractions of the gambling houses and saloons before selecting one of them for a fling. He strolled casually, glancing at the faces of the few men who were moving around at that early hour of the evening. But he saw no one familiar.

At each of the gambling houses he stepped through the door and stood motionless for a few moments, glancing quickly around at the few patrons who were bucking the games of chance. In all of them he entered—the Junction, the Lady Gay, the Crystal Palace, the Green Front, the Alhambra, the Long Branch, the Junction, the Lone Star— the results were much the same, there were more men at the bar in each of them than there were at all the table-games put together.

Ki was a bit discouraged when he entered the Oasis. It was the last of the deluxe gambling halls on the street, and he felt he'd have no better luck there than he'd had at the others. Only two of the green baize-covered poker tables had a full complement of players, at the third table the dealer was listlessly flipping cards to three hopefuls.

At both chuck-a-luck tables the cages hung motionless. One roulette wheel was still hidden by its black oilcloth dustcover. When he looked at the second table, where the wheel was still clicking as it spun, he saw only one man. The wheel stopped, the gambler shrugged and walked off.

Ki was about to turn away also when the croupier who'd been hidden by the loser reached with the rake to pull in the loser's stake. His eyes widened when he saw that the croupier was not only a woman, but an Oriental. Turning away from the door, Ki wove his way between the gaming tables to the roulette wheel.

As he neared the table the young woman croupier looked up at him and smiled an invitation. She gave the wheel a short spin. As Ki stopped across the table from her, he could tell at a glance that she was neither Japanese nor Chinese, but a mixture of Oriental and Anglo-Saxon blood.

"You will try your luck?" she asked, a half-question, half-statement.

"Perhaps. If you promise me it will be good."

"No." She shook her head. "Do not play unless you can afford to lose." Her English was almost as good as Ki's. Only a slight accent that turned her r's into l's betrayed her Oriental bloodstrain.

"You're honest," Ki told her.

"Perhaps not all the time, but to other Japanese I do not lie. Besides, the pit boss is not close enough to overhear us," she smiled.

Ki nodded and said, "Even from a distance I was sure that we are of the same blood."

"Yes," she nodded. "But please, if it is your wish to stay and talk you must give me a reason by risking a small sum. I cannot control what the wheel will do, it is an honest one. But if you are careful . . ."

"Of course," Ki replied. He reached into the slit pocket of his loose jacket and took out his purse. Fishing out a half-eagle, he laid it on the table in front of her.

"You can afford to lose this much?" she asked, her voice dropping to a half-whisper.

When Ki nodded, she pushed him a small stack of chips. He did not look to see their value, but placed two of them on the number in front of him. He kept his eyes on the girl and did not look to see the number.

She spun the wheel, then she leaned over the clacking ball, as close to him as possible, and said, "You are new in town. I know all of the Orientals here, and I have not seen you before."

Dropping his voice, Ki asked, "Have you been here in Dodge very long?"

"Too long, I'm afraid. Did you come from California?"

Ki shook his head. "No. From a ranch in Texas."

"Alone? You have a wife?"

Again Ki replied with a negative headshake, but before she could speak again the roulette wheel clicked to a stop. She glanced at the wheel, then turned to him.

"Your spin was good. Look, you've won." As she spoke she was adding more chips to the top of the small stack he'd wagered.

"What is your name?" Ki asked.

"Sumi. And you are?"

"Ki." When Sumi looked questioningly at him, he explained, "I do not use my family name. It is an old one, but I gave it up when I left my home after a dispute with my grandparents."

As she nodded her understanding, Sumi said, "You must spin again, Ki. The pit boss is looking this way."

Ki moved his swollen stack of chips to another number without taking his eyes off her. Then he said, "I am looking for a man named Blaise Caldwell, Sumi. Do you know him?"

"I know who he is," Sumi nodded. She spun the wheel again before going on, "He was here only last night."

"Gambling?"

She shook her head. "No. He and Whitey Norton talked for a long time at the bar. Then they went out together."

"Whitey Norton?" Ki frowned.

"A gunman. I think he's in some scheme with Caldwell." The wheel clicked to a stop. Sumi glanced at it and began to pile more chips on the already sizeable stack Ki had wagered. She told Ki, "Look, you've won again."

"You bring me good luck," Ki said. "And I think perhaps you can tell me things I need to know. Have you had supper?"

Sumi shook her head. "But the man who works at this wheel will be back soon. I only take his place when he goes out."

"Where can we eat and talk in private later on?"

For a long moment Sumi did not reply. Then she said, "I have food at home for my supper. There is enough for both of us. While we eat we can talk without being interrupted or overheard."

"If you're sure . . ."

"If I had any doubt, I would not invite you. But I must spin the wheel again, Ki. The man whose place I'm taking has just come in. Make another bet quickly, then cash in your chips and wait for me outside the front door."

"Dinner was delicious, Sumi," Ki told his hostess as they sat at the small round table in her flat. Supper was prolonged by conversation that allowed them to get better acquainted. "When I'm at the Circle Star, I cook a Japanese dish now and then for Jessie and myself, but I certainly can't match your skill."

"I'm glad," she replied. "I enjoyed sharing supper with you. There are too few Japanese here, Ki." She fixed her eyes on Ki's face and added, "I miss many pleasures of our homeland."

For a moment Ki wondered if he was interpreting Sumi's words and look correctly. When she maintained her unwavering gaze, he asked, "Pleasures shared by men and women, Sumi?"

"I was sure that you'd understand," she smiled. "Shall we go on with our sharing, Ki?"

"If you wish."

"Come with me, then," Sumi said.

Ki followed her into the adjoining room. It was unlighted except for the glow that came from the lamp in the room they'd just left, but Ki could see that the room was small and furnished in the sparse Japanese fashion. The room contained only three pieces of furniture: a long low cabinet filled one wall, a straight chair stood against the opposite wall, and instead of a bed the center of the room was dominated by a thick mattress that lay on the bare floor and was covered with a silken sheet.

After a quick glance around the shadowed chamber, Ki turned to Sumi. She had started to shed her clothes, and her dress fell to the floor. Then she bent to push her pantalets down her thighs. Her breasts had a fullness uncommon to women of the Far East and they swayed as she bent forward, their dark pink rosettes already pebbled, their tips protruding. In the Oriental custom, her pubic brush had been plucked to a pair of sparse thin lines.

Wasting no time, Ki followed Sumi's example. He skinned out of his blouse and loosened the sash that supported his widelegged trousers, letting them drop to the floor beside the blouse.

Sumi stepped up beside him, her hands moving at once to cradle his swelling erection. Ki had made no effort to remain lax. The sight of Sumi's creamy slender form, seeming to shimmer in the dim light, had aroused him quickly after his long abstinence at the ranch and during the trip.

"You are ready for me now," Sumi whispered. "Just as I am for you."

She sank backward on the mattress, pulling Ki with her. As his weight pressed down on her, Sumi guided him and sighed with pleasure as she felt him drive home. Ki did not begin to thrust at once, but held himself firmly against her as she started to rotate her hips and at the same time lift them to pull him even more deeply into her.

Sensing her pleasure, Ki held himself poised above her, filling her fully. She writhed in a gentle rhythm that slowly grew to a frenzied rocking, which started her slender body trembling. Then, suddenly, she stopped and held herself close to Ki, momentarily motionless.

"Can you hold on?" she whispered, looking up at Ki after her gasping breaths subsided.

"Yes, of course," Ki assured her. "Take your pleasure, Sumi. We will have all the time we need later to share each other. Make this your embrace instead of mine."

Sumi nodded as a deep sigh bubbled from her lips. Then she began the rhythmic rolling of her hips once more. She moved very slowly at first, and stopped completely several times. Ki remained motionless. He made no effort to thrust or to match Sumi's moves, letting her find gratification in her own way. Each time she slowed or stopped the gyrations of her hips he simply held himself poised, waiting for her to begin again.

At last Sumi increased the tempo of her rhythmic rolling movements. She was gasping now, her slender body trembling in recurrent waves, and Ki sensed that she was reaching a final climax. For the first time he began to bring his hips up to meet Sumi's. Now she wriggled more and more vigorously when lifting her buttocks.

She threw back her head, and her breathy sighs gave way to small throaty whimpers. In a few moments, her small mewling gasps followed one another with only a few seconds between them. Ki began lifting his hips faster and with greater force until the cries bubbled from Sumi's lips in a steady light staccato and her slim body began gyrating wildly.

Ki was soon thrusting with a vigor that matched Sumi's, bringing his hips up quickly and holding his rigid swollen shaft buried to the fullest. Sumi shook spastically and shuddered wildly until, with a final wrenching spasm, she collapsed and fell forward. He caught her and held her wrapped in his muscular arms until her writhing shudders faded to small quiverings that at last subsided, and she lay quietly.

"Did I please you well, Ki?" Sumi asked at last as she wriggled free of his arms. She raised her head and shoulders and lifted herself on her elbows to look down at him.

"Very well indeed. And you?"

"I'm happy and satisfied—but only for the moment—I do not often meet a man who pleases me as you do. And now that we are together, there are other ways we must explore."

"You mean the *o-so-kuzu-oe*?" Ki asked.

"Of course. They are my favorite studies."

"And you practice them as fully as you have studied them," he assured her.

"I've studied and practiced them enough to know that you did not join me in those last beautiful moments. You're still as big as ever. Now, I will give you the pleasure you denied yourself."

"Do, then," Ki told her. "And do not feel that you must hurry, Sumi. The night is still young, and there is no better way we can spend it than learning to know each other."

★

Chapter 11

"You moved very quietly when you came in this morning, Ki," Jessie said as they sat at breakfast in the hotel suite. "I listened for you last night until I fell asleep, and it was still dark when I woke up. Since you were so long in getting back, I know you must've run into something interesting."

"I did," Ki nodded. "I've opened a trail that may help us find Blaise Caldwell quicker than we'd have done otherwise."

"That's good news!" she exclaimed. As was always her custom, knowing that Ki would volunteer everything she should know about his activities, Jessie asked no questions but went on, "It's always good to have some strings out."

"Last night I met another Japanese who works at a gambling-house Caldwell seems to favor, one where he probably spends more time than he does here at the hotel. We'll know he's back here in Dodge as soon as he hits town."

"That's good news in more ways than one, then. From

124

what we know about his gambling habits, Blaise Caldwell may be in a big three-day poker game right now. We certainly can't be sure when he'll show up here at the hotel."

"It'll be better than going out ourselves and trying to track him down, Jessie. It's a chance to take Caldwell by surprise rather than risking him surprising us. If we get the jump on him, we'll be able to call the tune better."

"We can't catch him too soon to suit me. I want to find him before he can gamble away all the money he's stolen."

"If we have a bit of luck, we'll find him the next day or so," Ki told her. "That's not a promise, of course. But I can promise that we'll know right away when Caldwell shows up in what seems to be his regular stamping-grounds."

"What sort of arrangement did you make for us to get word from that gambling-house when Caldwell shows up?"

"A messenger. More than likely it'll be some down-and-outer who's never heard of us or knows anything about our reason for being here."

"Are you sure that will work out?" Jessie frowned. "What if there's a slip-up of some kind?"

"I don't see how there could be one. The messenger will know he'll get a good tip; I left the money for it with the desk clerk in a sealed envelope. And no matter which of the clerks is on duty, they'll send the message to one of us at once."

"I suppose that's the best arrangement possible."

"It has only one drawback that I can see," Ki went on. "It means that one of us will have to be here at the hotel all the time until Caldwell comes."

"That shouldn't be too hard to arrange. The only business we have here in Dodge is to run Caldwell to earth."

"I'm sure we'll manage," Ki nodded. "Now, unless you

need me for something, I'm going to catch up on my lost sleep."

"As long as you're going to be here, I'll go out and get a breath of fresh air," Jessie told him. "Just a short walk around town, maybe out to the end of Main Street. You know I always like to do that, especially in a place we haven't visited for quite a while. I'll only be gone . . . oh, twenty or thirty minutes."

Ki nodded. "Fine. And unless something happens in the meantime, when I wake up we can work out some kind of schedule that'll keep one of us here in case Caldwell should stop by the hotel when he gets back from wherever he is."

Jessie left for her stroll, and Ki made a beeline for his room. Stretching out without bothering to turn back the covers of his bed, he was asleep within a few seconds.

Dodge City's Main Street in the light of the dawning day was a great deal different from its aspect at night, and the difference struck Jessie at once as she paused outside the hotel door and looked along the wide gravelled thoroughfare.

At that hour of the day the street, which during the night had been alive with men moving from one saloon or gambling hall to another, was almost deserted. There were only a few vehicles in sight, three big four-horse hitch freight-carriers lumbering along with empty wagon beds and a small one-horse delivery cart bouncing over the ruts. Here and there along the street saddled horses stood patiently at the hitch-rails in front of the saloons, waiting for riders to finish their morning wake-up nip.

Although lights still showed in the windows and through the open doors of the saloons and gambling palaces, the blazing acetylene lights above them had been extinguished, and without their brilliant glare the palaces of pleasure looked a bit dowdy.

A few of them glistened with fresh paint, making the facades of their neighbors appear dull and weather-beaten. Virtually all of the windows that faced the street were in need of washing. Paths of rain-streaks gave them the appearance of the face of an elderly hag who'd just woken up and had not yet applied the disguising veneer of rouge and powder.

Jessie was in no hurry. She strolled leisurely, avoiding the few men who came blear-eyed from a night of gambling in the houses of chance and the shuttered bawdy-houses. Now and then she took a few steps into a side street to look into the windows of an early-opening store, or paused on Main Street to glance into one of the few stores that were widely-spaced between the gaming-places and saloons. Most of the small retail establishments were open, and she poked into one or two of these. But the hour was still too early for many of them; their doors were locked and their windows shuttered.

Main Street changed character instantly as Jessie reached the last of the gambling-spots. Beyond a narrow strip of open land the red-light district stood, a couple of acres of small shanties and several row-houses with their front doors cheek by jowl. Paths rather than streets or alleys wound in streaks of boot-beaten earth between the small structures where the glow of red lanterns fought a losing battle with the brightening day.

There was a wide swathe of open land between the district and the freighters' stables and sheds, which were bordered by wide strips of raw prairie on all sides. Beyond the open area on each side the scattered houses of Dodge

City's permanent residents arced and merged gradually with the grid of streets forming the town's center.

Jessie paused at the beginning of the red-light district and turned back to look at the town. She was just beginning to start for the hotel when a shrill scream came from one of the nearby shanties, then a woman burst from the door of one of the cribs. She wore only a long tissue-thin chemise that trailed in puffs behind her as she ran. She was still screaming when she saw Jessie and started toward her.

"I got to have some help," she panted as she came closer to Jessie. "There's a wild drunk in my crib back there! He's got a big ugly knife, and he says he's going to cut me up just like he would a slab of bacon!"

"I'd say the best thing for you to do is stay away, then," Jessie advised. She looked at the woman's thin dress, which did nothing to hide the dark rosettes of her bulging breasts or the dark triangle at the vee of her thighs. "Even if you're not really dressed for it, you'd better go into town and get the constable to come out and arrest the man who's threatening you."

"Listen, lady, Nat Haywood's the constable, and he ain't about to lift his little pinkie finger to help one of us crib-house girls. Maybe you don't know the rules he's laid down. One of 'em is that any of us that works out here and wants to go into town has got to be dressed decent."

"Surely that wouldn't mean you, not if you're in trouble and need *help*!"

"Nat don't know that word for the likes of us," the woman said. "When I seen you here I figured between us we might get that john in my crib to just go away and leave me alone. I'd sure be thankful to you if you'd help me."

"Well . . ." Jessie said hesitantly, "I suppose we women have to stand together."

"I'll sure be thankful to you if you just would."

Jessie had been careful to tuck her Colt into her purse before leaving the hotel. Opening the bag she took out the revolver as she said, "I'll go with you and try to talk some sense into the man who's giving you trouble."

Walking side by side, the two women started for the crib. The door of the ramshackle unpainted shanty stood open, but all that Jessie could see of its dark interior was one corner of the footboard of a bed. She took a step to one side, but still could make out nothing.

"You inside there!" she called, "I've got a gun and know how to use it! Now come out of there and make yourself scarce!" There was no reply from the deeply shadowed interior, and after a moment had passed, Jessie tried again.

"Come on out, now! All you have to do is step through the door and keep walking!"

"Maybe that fellow's passed out, he was drunk enough to," the woman suggested. "But I'm still afraid to go inside all by myself. Would you feel like coming in with me?"

"It looks like I'll have to, unless that man shows himself or comes out," Jessie frowned. "Drunks do strange things."

"He was sure drunk enough to drop off," her companion said. "But I'm still afeared to go in by myself."

"I'll go with you," Jessie offered. "Just watch the door closely, and if that man comes out shooting, drop flat on the ground."

Slowly they approached the dark yawning doorway. A single step took them to the narrow porch that ran across the little shanty's facade. Though Jessie watched vigilantly, she could see no movement inside. She moved to the door, raising her Colt as a precaution as she neared the dark rectangle.

Jessie was not prepared for what followed. Suddenly, she felt the hands of the woman who'd called for help dig into her back and push vigorously. Propelled forward through the door, Jessie staggered ahead, her arms flailing as she tried to keep her balance. Then, before she could fall, a man's strong arm closed around her to pin her upper arms to her body, and a hamlike hand knocked the Colt from her grasp. The revolver hit the floor with a thud as the man closed a rough hand over her mouth.

In spite of the unexpected attack, Jessie kept cool. She tried to twist free of the arm that was hugging her to the chest of the man who was holding her, but his strength was great enough to defeat her efforts.

"You might as well give up," he said. His lips were close enough to Jessie's head for her to smell the liquor on his breath as he spoke. He went on, "Now you can do either one of two things. You can hold still and keep quiet while I tie you up. Or you can keep this up till I gotta drop this hand I got on your mouth and grab you by the neck and choke you till you pass out. And you just might not wake up at all, if I got to do that!"

"Wait a minute, Whitey!" the woman who'd lured Jessie into the trap protested. "You said there wasn't gonna be no bad rough stuff! Damn you for a lying son-of-a-bitch! You kill that lady in my crib, and I'll have to start running from the law!"

"Shut up, Ruby!" Whitey snapped. "I ain't supposed to kill her, but this damn dame's fighting like a she-bear!"

Jessie took advantage of the distraction to kick backward, trying to land a boot-heel on her captor's shin and at

130

the same time renewing her struggle to break free of his encircling grip. As strong as she was, she could not budge the muscular arm that immobilized her own arms, and her kicking foot flailed into empty air.

Now the man called Whitey spoke again, "Damn you, Ruby, don't stand there like you lost your good sense! Grab one of them rags off of your wash-stand there and put a gag on this bitch while I hold her! While you're at it, you better tie her hands in behind her back, too. And if you know what's good for you, you'll do it fast!"

Jessie heard Ruby's feet pattering across the uncarpeted board floor, and in a moment the crib-whore stepped in front of her holding some threadbare strips of white toweling. Jessie saw there was nothing she could do alone against the two of them. She stood quietly while Ruby bound her wrists together, but when the woman stepped around with another length of the fabric and lifted it to her face, Jessie drew back and tried to pull away.

"Now, you don't need to worry," Ruby said. "It's a clean rag, ain't been used on a trick a-tall. Now, I guess you've found out how mean Whitey is, so don't get yourself hurt trying to fight him while I put this gag on you."

Recognizing the soundness of Ruby's advice, Jessie let the woman tie the gag around her mouth without a struggle. Ruby stepped back when she'd secured the knot and turned to Whitey.

"I want my pay for this job right now," she said. "I done a lot more'n I was supposed to, and I got a hunch there's gonna be trouble about this woman sooner or later. I don't aim to get caught up in it."

Whitey's grating voice was rougher than usual as he

growled, "Soon as I hand her over to the boss and he pays me, you'll get your split and not before."

"You said he'd be here right away," Ruby protested. "If I'd've had any sense I'd've done you and him like I do my tricks and got the cash on the line first!"

Another man's voice broke in before Whitey could reply. He said, "Don't worry, Ruby. You'll get whatever Whitey promised you."

Jessie tried to swivel around to see the newcomer, but Whitey's grip tightened on her arms the instant he felt her begin an effort to move. The man who'd spoken was standing in the doorway, blocking out the morning light that was flooding through it and throwing the cramped interior of the little crib-house into dimness.

"It's about time you was getting here, Blaise Caldwell!" Ruby said angrily. "I still don't know what all it is you and Whitey's up to this time, but it sure smells like big trouble if the law catches up to you."

"Whatever trouble comes along, I'll handle it, just like I have before," Caldwell replied. "And stop worrying, damn it! You'll be paid, just like always."

"Settle up with her now, Blaise," Whitey urged. "You're later than you said you'd be, and pretty soon there'll be somebody coming to the row to start the day off right."

"I had to wait a long time at the livery stable, while they got the landau ready and hitched up," Caldwell said. "I'm not fool enough to try carrying her through Dodge in a buggy. The landau's right outside, at the end of the row. You take the Starbuck woman down there and load her into it. I'll square up with Ruby and be right along."

"Maybe you better give me a hand while we tie her feet," Whitey told Caldwell. "This damn dame's strong as

132

a man, and I don't aim to have to chase her. Folks in town'll be up and about by now, and somebody'd be bound to see us."

"I suppose you're right," Caldwell agreed. "Push her down across the bed and hold her still."

Jessie tried to kick free of Whitey's hands as he pushed her facedown across Ruby's tousled bed, but without the use of her hands she had no chance to break away. She lay with her face pressed into the tousled bedding, which was sour with the stink of old sweat, while they tied her ankles together.

Helpless now, she found her limited struggles useless as Caldwell and Whitey levered her across Whitey's shoulders, and he carried her like a sack out of the cribhouse and down to the road, where he opened the door of the closed carriage that had been pulled off the road at the end of the row of shanties.

Whitey was opening the landau's door when Jessie heard a muffled gunshot from the direction of the cribs. Her anger burned bitterly, for she knew that Caldwell had just gotten rid of a witness to his crimes. But there was nothing she could do about it. She relaxed to cushion her fall as Whitey leaned forward and dumped her on the floor of the carriage, then she heard its door close.

After what seemed a very long time, she felt the landau swaying as Caldwell and his accomplice climbed up to the high outside seat. Then there was a jolt as the carriage moved away, heading for a destination at which Jessie could not even guess, any more than she could fathom the reason why Caldwell and the man she knew only as Whitey were kidnapping her.

● ● ●

Sunlight striking his eyes from the slit between the window shade and its casing woke Ki with a start. He lay quietly for a moment, listening for movements from the suite's living room. He heard nothing. He glanced at the slit-like lines of sunlight on the bed and on the floor, and from the distance between their tips and the window-slits they shone through, he could tell that the morning was well along.

Ki lay quietly, his ears attuned. When not even a whisper of hushed sound broke the room's stillness he rolled off the bed, dressed hurriedly, and stepped into the room which lay between his bedroom and Jessie's. The room was just as he'd left it.

Ki moved to the door of Jessie's room and tapped, lightly at first, then harder. When the raps of his knuckles brought no response, he opened the door. Emptiness and silence greeted him. Ki glanced around. The room showed all the signs of Jessie's occupancy, which he'd long ago become familiar with due to their many trips together. Her saddlebags leaned against the wall; her silk lounging robe was draped across a chair; the hairbrush, comb, and silver powderbox of her traveling toiletries kit, which had been her last gift from Alex Starbuck, lay on the dresser.

Puzzled now, a germ of worry forming in his mind, Ki stepped back into the connecting room. It looked just as it had when he and Jessie parted earlier in the day. Nothing had been moved. Worried now, Ki went downstairs to the lobby.

"Miss Starbuck left the hotel some time ago," he said to the room clerk. "I'm sure you must have seen her go out."

"Yes, I did," the man replied. "I was on duty when she left, but she hasn't come back yet. I've been here at the

134

desk all the time. I'd certainly have seen her if she'd come in."

"Thank you," Ki nodded. "If she comes in while I'm gone, tell her that I'll be back very soon."

His worry and puzzlement increasing by the minute, Ki went outside and made his way to the livery stable behind the hotel. The same grizzled liveryman who had been on duty when he and Jessie rode in was grooming a horse in front of the open doors of the stable. Glancing past him into the stable, Ki saw the familiar rumps of the horses he and Jessie had rented in Coffeyville for their ride to Medicine Lodge.

"I don't suppose you've seen Miss Starbuck this morning?" Ki asked the liveryman.

"Sure ain't. Far as I know, she ain't come out here since her and you got to town yestiddy."

"You've been here all the time?"

"Sure have. Got routed up early, fellow that's a regular customer from the hotel wanted t'rent a big closed rig for a trip he was gonna make. We only got one big landau, and we been trying to fix up a busted spring on it. I had t'finish fixing it up, and he made me sorta nervous, he did, standing around like he was bossing the job and telling me how big a hurry he was in."

"Thank you," Ki nodded. "If Miss Starbuck should come in or even pass by the stable here, please tell her that I will return soon."

"Be glad to oblige," the grizzled oldster replied. "You want I should get your nag saddled up?"

"Not now," Ki told him. "Perhaps later."

Turning away from the stable, Ki walked through the alley to Main Street. His face was sober, his forehead creased. He looked at the street, abustle now with the business of the day.

His eyes fell on the windows of the building across the street and suddenly Ki realized that in his preoccupation with the mystery of Jessie's whereabouts he had neglected to ask the one key question that might give him a clue. He turned and hurried back into the hotel.

★

Chapter 12

During the few minutes since he'd had left the hotel lobby, another desk clerk had taken the place of the man Ki had questioned earlier. Stopping at the desk, he asked, "The man who was here a few minutes ago, can you tell me where he is now?"

"More'n likely he's gone to the kitchen. We almost always have a bite to eat after we get off," the new clerk replied.

"Where is the kitchen?"

"Why, it's downstairs in the basement, but guests aren't allowed—"

When he realized that he was speaking into empty air the desk clerk stopped short. The moment Ki heard the word "kitchen" he'd started at a run toward the staircase. He took the steps two at a time and pushed through the glass-paned swinging doors. At that time of day the kitchen was abustle as the cooks and their flunkies prepared for the noon meal.

Coming to a halt just inside the big busy room, Ki looked around for a moment before he saw the man he was looking for. The clerk was seated alone at a small table in the rear, away from the confusion that prevailed elsewhere. Ki hurried to the table. The clerk looked up from his plate when Ki stopped beside him.

"There is one question which I overlooked asking you when we were talking upstairs," Ki said. "Did Blaise Caldwell come in last night?"

"Not during the night, he didn't," the clerk replied. He spoke with difficulty, his mouth half-full. Chewing rapidly, he gulped and went on, "It was an hour or so before sunup when he came in. And I didn't forget about what Miss Starbuck asked me to do. I didn't say a word about you and her being here, but I had it in mind to go upstairs before I went home and tell her that Mr. Caldwell's come back."

"Never mind that now," Ki said, controlling his impatience and keeping his voice calmly level. "Did Caldwell go to his room?"

"No." The clerk speared another morsel of meat on his fork as he shook his head. "He said he had something to take care of at the livery stable before he went upstairs."

"Did he stay out there very long?"

"Come to think of it, I didn't see him when he came back. He must've gone past the desk while I was busy."

"Thank you," Ki nodded as he started to turn away. "You've helped me a great deal."

Before the clerk could say anything more, Ki was on his way back to the stairs. He hurried to the stable, where he found the old liveryman still working at his grooming job.

"You told me about fixing up a carriage, a big closed

landau, for a customer who was in a hurry," Ki said. "Would your customer have been Blaise Caldwell?"

"Now, how'd you find that out?" the hostler asked. "It was him, all right, but I don't recall saying so when you and me was talking a little bit ago."

"I've been looking for Caldwell as well as Miss Starbuck," Ki replied. "You didn't happen to see them together, did you?"

"Can't say as I did. Not today nor any other time," the oldster frowned.

"You're sure that she didn't leave in the landau with Caldwell?" Ki persisted.

"Why, I can't say yes or no about that."

"But Caldwell did go off in the landau?" Ki insisted.

"Sure. Headed toward Main Street. I wasn't right sure about how the leaf I had t'put in that spring was gonna behave, so I walked along behind him to the street to watch it when he druv away."

"You saw him turn into Main Street, then?"

"I did, for a fact," the liveryman nodded. "And the spring was behavin' jest fine. After he turned into the street, I figured I'd done the job all right, so I come on back."

"Which way did he go when he turned at Main Street?"

"Towards the river. What's all this fuss about, anyways?"

Ki ignored the question and asked another of his own. "How could I recognize that landau if I saw it?"

"Well, hell, mister! It's just like any other one I ever seen. Sorta square-boxy, little windows on both sides of the door. Doors has got windows, too. Seat for the driver's on the roof of the body, and—" The liveryman stopped short. A frown had formed on his face while he talked to Ki, and now he asked again, "How come you're so interested in that rig?"

"Never mind," Ki replied. He was fingering the coins in his pocket as he spoke. When he identified a half-eagle by its size he took it out and held it where the liveryman could see it before he went on, "Just one more question. What color is that landau painted?"

His eyes fixed on the gold piece, the liveryman answered, "It's done up in a sorta sandy tan. Dark brown trim."

"Thank you," Ki said. He handed the liveryman the gold coin and went on, "Now, if you'll just saddle Miss Starbuck's horse and mine, I'll be back for them in about ten or fifteen minutes."

"Be glad to," the liveryman smiled, fingering the half-eagle. "Now if you got any more questions, jest trot 'em out and I'll sure be glad to answer 'em."

Ki said, "Thank you, but I believe I've found out all I can hope for. If I think of something else, I'll ask you."

Hurrying up to the suite he and Jessie had occupied, Ki had their saddlebags packed in ten minutes. He stopped at the desk long enough to settle their account, then hurried to the livery stable. The two horses were saddled and waiting. He knotted the reins of Jessie's horse to the girth-strap of his saddle and mounted. Then he toed the horse ahead and with Jessie's mount following reined his horse onto Main Street.

Dodge City was fully awake by now. The street was busy, crowded with rigs of every sort and men on horseback moving beside and between them, pedestrians weaving in and out, crossing the street and walking along the board sidewalks.

Ki flicked his eyes over the sidewalks now and then, as

well as on the wheel-rutted hoof-pocked street, even though he was sure that he'd see nothing of interest until he'd gotten out of town. He rode past the business section, the gambling houses, the cribs, and the cemetery to where the road's deep dust had fewer wheel-ruts and hoofprints.

Though Ki realized that his suspicions might be groundless, his idea an illusion, it was the only course that he could see to follow in his search. He kept his eyes on the road, trying to pick out the freshest wheel-tracks.

Once he'd passed the empty idle buildings of Fort Dodge the wheel-ruts were fewer and clearer. As he rode steadily on, Ki paid closer attention to them. Now, where a smaller number of wagons had passed over the road, individual sets of the fresher ruts could be distinguished more clearly.

Ki was beginning by now to recognize with very few mistakes the sets of parallel ruts made by each individual vehicle that had passed over the road recently. He was having trouble picking out the wheel-ruts of the landau, however. It was lighter in weight than the big cargo wagons, even lighter than the small short-haul wagons when they were loaded. Apparently, the landau had passed over the road ahead of the freight wagons, for their wheel-ruts crossed and recrossed its shallow tracks, in many stretches almost obliterating the landau's tracks.

In spite of the difficulty he encountered, Ki persisted. After a few miles he began to become familiar with the small variation in every rut, for each iron tire on the different and various vehicles had its own characteristics. Not only were there slight differences in the width of each tire, but all of them had a wide range of individual flaws to give them their own identity.

Some of the broad thick iron rims had cracks along their

141

edges, nicks, rough spots, hammer-scars, or incised parallel lines from the handling tongs of the blacksmiths who'd put on the tires. All these slight differences helped him to identify the different wagons, and soon he had tucked into his memory the patterns that marked the edges and faces of each strap-iron tire on each wheel of all the heavy freight wagons.

Each flaw or scar on each wheel left an individual imprint in the dust and was repeated with every revolution of the wheel. The iron tires of smaller farm wagons and carts had their own characteristic cracks and blemishes, as did the less frequent sets of narrow ruts made by buggies. Any other tracker with skill equal to Ki's who studied the thick layer of dust on the road would have been as quick as Ki to identify and trace the course of a specific wagon or cart or buggy.

By the time he'd reached the ford called Mulberry Crossing, where the Arkansas River ran shallow and—at the moment—clear, Ki had not been able to identify the landau's tracks. Reining in when he reached the water's edge, he dismounted to study the wheel-prints in the road more closely while the horses drank. Here the river shoaled to a depth of only a few inches, and its bank curved away from the road in a wide crescent, running down to the water in a long gentle slope.

Most of the soil on the slope was barren, but it was broken here and there by patches of short, thin-growing grass through which the ground was plainly visible. A majority of the wagon-tracks ran down the center of the arc to the water's edge, a wide area that was cut and criss-crossed by wheel-ruts and pock-marked by the hooves of many mules and horses.

Leaving his mount and the other horse to drink, Ki

glanced upstream and saw a short stretch where the earth was smoother and shortgrass ran to within a yard or less of the water's edge. To get a drink for himself and to save the limited amount of water in his canteen, he walked to the grassy strip and hunkered down. He cupped his hand and was bending forward to scoop up some water when he saw the small pointed boot-track on the river-bottom.

Though the indentation's outlines just beyond the water's edge were already being eroded by the gentle backwash of the current, there was enough of its original shape left to enable Ki to recognize it at once. He'd seen too many identical prints in other places to be mistaken. It was the print of one of Jessie's favorite bench-made boots.

Forgetting the water he'd scooped up, Ki rose and began an inch-by-inch search of the grassy area leading away from the riverbank. At the water's edge, downstream from the footprint, he discovered the almost invisible ruts left by a vehicle that had wheel-tracks too wide to have been made by a buggy and too narrow and shallow to have been made by a heavy wagon. The shortgrass stems that had been crushed by the wheels were already straightening up. Within another two hours or so, Ki could tell that they would be invisible.

"It's the landau, of course," he muttered, his voice just above a whisper. "So Blaise Caldwell must've captured Jessie."

In spite of his instinctive urge to hurry and catch up with the landau, Ki's many experiences during the years following Alex's death when they were battling the sinister foreign cabal had taught him to make haste slowly.

He backtracked the landau's faint wheel-ruts across the grass until he reached the relatively track-clear spot where it had been pulled off the road. In the narrow strip of smooth soil between the road and the grass-covered crescent he finally came to a strip of bare earth that held a clean-cut set of all four of the landau's wheel-marks.

Ki studied them carefully for several minutes, until he was positive that he'd memorized the two or three special marks which would make his tracking easier. A rim on one wheel had a V at one edge that left a triangle in the dust. Another rim was distinguished by a short sharp knifelike strip protruding from the edge. A third track bore a V-shaped indentation made by an extra strong blow of the blacksmith's hammer when he trued the edges.

At last Ki was sure that he could identify at a glance the bumps, nicks and scars that set the landau's iron tires apart from any tracks made by another buggy or farm wagon. Only then did he begin searching for other evidence that Jessie's captors had indeed stopped there. His scouting was less than successful. There were edge-muffled footprints here and there, but all these traces there were too scattered and too faint to be of any help.

Satisfied that his discoveries would be enough to enable him to pick up and follow the landau's wheel-marks, Ki hurried back to the horses. He mounted and returned to the rutted road. Now he pressed ahead at a faster clip, positive that he'd found the trail he'd been seeking, and resolved not to lose it.

Ki's hunger grew as he rode through the sunlit afternoon, but the urge to hurry overcame his stomach's protests. He pushed ahead, ignoring hunger, taking a sip or two from the canteen without reining in, stopping only to let the horses drink when they began showing signs of thirst. Strangely, he'd not as yet encountered any of the wagons that he'd confidently expected to see heading for Dodge. At last he came upon one, and the wagoner reined in and waved. Taking the wave as an invitation for him to stop, Ki pulled up.

"Road's all right up ahead, I guess?" the man in the other wagon asked.

"Yes," Ki replied. "But there's not much moving on it."

"Freight train ain't due in Dodge till day after tomorrow," the other said. "Road'll be full tomorrow. I ain't one to buck a bunch of other rigs, so I allus come in a day early."

"Did you happen to pass a tan landau heading east?" Ki asked.

"Nope. Ain't seen any rig since I hit the fork."

"There's a fork ahead?" Ki frowned.

"Why, sure. Guess you don't know much about this road, or you wouldn't be having to ask."

"I don't know it at all. If you'd give me an idea of what's ahead, I'd appreciate it."

"Now, the main road follows up north along the big bend in the Arkansas. The branch road goes down into the Indian Nation."

Ki's spirits were higher now. He asked, "I suppose the south branch road is as good as the north one?"

"Good enough, I reckon. Sorta lonesome, but passable. It don't git much use now, ain't had a lot since the damn railroads begun hauling freight faster'n we can in our wagons."

"Thank you," Ki nodded. "Now I'd better push on, but I'll know what to look for up ahead."

"No thanks needed," the old teamster replied. "See you next time we meet."

With a wave, Ki toed his horse ahead.

• • •

145

When she was thrown into the landau by Whitey, Jessie's head had landed with a solid thwack on the thinly upholstered armrest that protruded above the seat. The impact was not hard enough to knock her unconscious, but it stunned her lightly and kept her lying limp during the few minutes required for Caldwell and his accomplice to get the vehicle into motion.

Full awareness returned bit by bit. Jessie struggled to a sitting position, but after a few minutes the strain on her wrists, lashed together as they were behind her back, forced her to drop into a position that was half-sitting, half-lying on the vehicle's seat.

Realizing that she could do nothing with the bonds on her arms and legs, Jessie began working on the strip of cloth with which she'd been gagged. Though she pressed at it with her tongue and tried to chew it apart, she had no more success with it than she'd with her other fetters. She gave up for the moment and wriggled around until she found a position that was almost comfortable, then forced herself to relax.

As Jessie reclined she took stock of the interior of the carriage. The first thing she noted was that each of the wide upholstered seats at the front and rear of the spacious vehicle would accommodate two passengers in luxurious comfort and three with a minimum of cramping. Thick pile carpeting covered the floor. Silk curtains were drawn over the small windows set in the sides above each seat and in the top half of the doors.

Jessie had no idea how long she'd lain semiconscious. She lifted her head, trying to look outside, but found that while enough light came through the sheer fabric to make the interior cheerfully bright, the silken curtains prevented anyone from seeing through them. No matter how hard she strained to look through the windows, objects on the outside were visible only as blurred shapes.

Fully conscious now, Jessie began to think of escape. She tested her bonds again, but the strips of fabric clung to her wrists more closely than rope. She could twist and bend her wrists enough to feel the knots with her fingertips, but could not tell merely by the limited scope allowed her feeling how the knots that secured her wrist-bonds could be untied.

In her half-reclining position, her head and body lying on the seat and her legs trailing down to the floor, she could not see the strips of cloth that bound her ankles. In spite of her bonds, Jessie began trying to change her position to see if she could free her feet. At least, she told herself as she began wriggling around, she'd be able to inspect the bonds around her ankles to see if she could twist and bend to reach them. With her legs freed she could leap from the wagon and dash away. If she was lucky as well as fast, she might be able to elude her captors.

Her efforts were halted almost before they began. The landau had been rolling along at a good clip, now it slowed and stopped before she could begin her efforts to free her feet. The carriage swayed briefly, then the door opened and Blaise Caldwell swung inside.

"Well, Miss Starbuck," he said. "You've certainly played the devil with my plans. I'm sure you realize you're going to have to pay for that."

Jessie kept her eyes on Caldwell's face, getting her first look at the man she and Ki had been pursuing. There was nothing really remarkable about his features, though his jaw was shorter and more rounded than was normal for a man in his late thirties or early forties. His cheeks were puffy and his nose thin, giving his face an appearance of petulance. His eyes were a very pale blue, almost color-less.

Her fixed stare had the effect she'd intended. Caldwell shifted nervously on the seat, then turned his head away for a moment. When he faced her again he avoided her effort to lock her eyes onto his for a second time by moving his head and turning away from her every few seconds while he spoke.

"Yes," he went on, "from what my father told me about the Starbuck industrial empire that your father built, I realized at once that I couldn't offer you a bribe large enough to keep you silent."

Jessie gave no indication that she'd heard, but continued her efforts to lock Caldwell's eyes again. After several instances of either lowering his head or turning it away to prevent their eyes from locking, he pulled out the large silk handkerchief that puffed from the breast pocket of his jacket, then shook out its folds and draped it over her head, in effect blinding her.

"I was sure from your reputation, and from that of your father's, that you must've come to collect on that note when I learned of your arrival in Medicine Lodge," he went on. "And when the posse you and your man were with caught those clumsy fools I'd hired to rob the bank, I began worrying. Luckily, the good citizens of the town saved me the trouble of having to get rid of my hired hands myself, but I killed a very fine specimen of horseflesh racing to Dodge City."

Again Caldwell paused. Jessie was sure of what he was leading up to in his circuitious chatter, but she remained motionless. She heard the scratching of a match, then caught a whiff of smoke from the cigar she now knew Caldwell had lighted.

148

"I can see now that I made a mistake when I ran from you," he went on. "It doesn't bother me a bit to admit that. And I'll also admit that I made a mistake some time earlier, when I wrote you that letter. You see, I'd heard a great deal about you from my father, and I hoped the letter would keep you from traveling all the way from Texas to Medicine Lodge, but it seems to've had the opposite effect. And I certainly didn't anticipate that you'd pick up my trail to Dodge so quickly."

Again Caldwell paused to puff his cigar, then he said in a tone that was quietly casual but no less determined, "I'm sure you understand what I'm getting at, Miss Starbuck. I have no alternative now but to kill you."

★

Chapter 13

Jessie had been anticipating Blaise Caldwell's threat. She'd heard similar threats before and even if her face had not been covered she'd have had all the self-control required to keep from showing any emotion.

Caldwell went on, "Don't worry. Whitey is an expert shot, and you'll die quickly when the time comes. But there is one, perhaps I should say two things that he and I have agreed on before then. You have a great deal of charm, Miss Starbuck. In fact, you're a very beautiful woman, and Whitey and I have both been very greatly attracted to you. I'll be first, of course, then I'll see that Whitey doesn't treat you too roughly."

Jessie had realized from the moment of her capture that she could expect no mercy from Caldwell. However, she hadn't anticipated this new development.

When Caldwell stopped speaking a fresh gust of cigar smoke drifted through the kerchief covering Jessie's head.

She waited for him to continue, and after a long moment of silence passed, he picked up his rambling discourse.

"That will have to wait until we stop for the night," he said. "But afterwards there'll still be two more full days of travel ahead. I advise you to enjoy them."

Caldwell said nothing when he'd finished his long rambling threat. Jessie was forced by the chafing gag and her bonds to keep silent and motionless while the words she might have used in response to his malice-laden expositions raced around in her mind. She waited, wondering about the reason for his long sillence, trying to anticipate something he could add to the threats he'd already uttered.

Apparently Caldwell shared Jessie's inability to think of anything more. She heard his knuckles rapping on the landau's roof and felt the carriage swaying to a halt again as Whitey reined in the horse. The carriage had not yet stopped swaying gently when the door-latch clicked.

Then full daylight struck Jessie's eyes as Caldwell grabbed the handkerchief from her head and stepped out. During the long period when Jessie's eyes had been shielded, they'd gotten widely dilated, and the sudden brightness caused them to water. She got only a blurred glimpse of Caldwell as he slammed the door shut, and in a moment the now familiar swaying vibration that accompanied the landau's movement resumed.

As Ki progressed along the trail, the wagon-tracks that had been so plentiful between Dodge City and the first ford across the Arkansas at Fort Dodge grew more and more scarce. They were no longer intertwined into an almost undecipherable pattern that earlier had turned the road's dusty surface into a maze. Now each individual set of shallow ruts took on its own identity and the narrower iron tires of the landau stood out from the rest.

Skilled as he was in reading trail-signs, Ki realized that with the trail so clear he could now move faster. He covered several miles along the river-trail before encountering another wide swathe of wheel-ruts running down to the water, and he knew the instant he saw them that he'd now reached the beginning of the stream's second great bend.

Ki paid no attention to the road's north fork, knowing that it led to the half-dozen forts that were scattered along the Arkansas's tributaries. He spent a few minutes making sure that the landau had indeed continued along the southern fork. The very fact that it had done so sent Ki an important message: Caldwell had not anticipated such swift pursuit. Sure now that the landau could not be too far ahead, Ki toed his horse to a faster pace as he followed the wheel-tracks on the southern branch of the road.

Though he'd solved the most immediate problem he'd been facing, Ki's frustration with his slow progress had not ended but had intensified after passing the fork of the road.

He could not push aside the thought that he was not moving swiftly enough as the horses he and Jessie had rented moved along the rougher and stonier lesser-used branch of the trace. The livery-trained animals were not accustomed to long fast rides across the rugged river bottom terrain. They did not accept the hard going as a ranch-trained horse would have done. On the rougher trail they'd now taken both animals proved to be much less tractable than the carefully broken-in Circle Star horses to which he was accustomed.

After the led horse had bumped roughly into Ki's mount two or three times, it was apparent to him that the animal was not one that adjusted easily to being led instead of ridden. It kept trying to catch up with Ki's mount and gallop ahead of it, and the lead-rope was not long enough to give the horse the slack required for it to do so. Each time its lead drew taut and slowed its progress, the animal began to dance and rear and shy into the horse Ki was riding.

Ki's patience was considerable, but he grew tired of having his pace slowed by the captious animal. He reined in and added a spare hame-strap to the lead-rope to lengthen it. Once the riderless mount found that it could stay neck-and-neck with its companion it stopped its efforts to catch up and adapted to the even pace set by the other animal.

Now Ki could push ahead without losing precious time in attending to a stubborn horse. He kept moving at the swiftest gait he dared maintain without danger of blowing or foundering the animals. However, the hours he'd spent in the saddle had by now begun to tell on even Ki's well-conditioned muscles. Worse than that, he became acutely aware of the reminders that his stomach was sending him almost constantly: a message that it had received no food at all since he first woke up that morning.

Even though he was positive that when he and Jessie got to Dodge City he'd emptied his saddlebags of all the trail victuals that he'd been carrying, and though he was positive that he'd gotten rid of everything edible, Ki rummaged through the saddlebags to confirm that his certainty was correct. Then he wondered if Jessie might not have overlooked doing the same minor task.

Slowing the horses to a walk, he leaned over to the mount Jessie had been riding and explored the saddlebag nearest him. Luck favored him at last, even though it was in a small way. He found the oilskin-wrapped packet in which Jessie carried her supply of trail-food.

When unwrapped, the little parcel yielded the wrinkled drying remnants of a piece of prospector's bread, a twist of boiled ham and a small triangle of rock-hard cheese. Ki toed his horse ahead again and after getting well under way he coiled its reins around his saddle horn. Without slowing his progress, he nibbled at the food, taking small bites and chewing thoroughly until not a remnant remained.

Jessie was not too greatly surprised when the landau came to a halt and Blaise Caldwell opened the door, stepped in quickly, and settled down on the seat across from her. This time he made no move to cover her face, but sat and stared fixedly at her for several moments before he spoke.

"I suppose that by now you've figured out where we're going," he said. His voice was casual, almost friendly, as he went on, "Now that there's no danger of anyone overhearing you, let me relieve you of your gag."

Bending forward, Caldwell worked at the knotted strip of cloth until its ends fell free, then lifted it away. He asked again, "You do know where we're going, I'd imagine?"

Her voice cold, Jessie parried his question. She replied, "Aren't you forgetting that I've been tied up here for the better part of a day, with the windows screened?"

"So you have," Caldwell replied. Now his tone was mocking. He went on, "Perhaps you'll be surprised when I tell you that we're heading back to Medicine Lodge."

Jessie was in full control of her features this time. She showed no surprise, even as a possible reason flashed into her mind.

"Why would you want to do that?" she asked.

"Call it unfinished business, Miss Starbuck. Business that I'd planned to complete, and quite probably would have been able to conclude, except for you and your oriental friend sticking your noses into my affairs so unexpectedly."

"When your affairs, as you call them, involve a great deal of my money, I make it a point to investigate them," Jessie told him. Her voice was still calmly level.

"Why would you possibly need more money?" Caldwell frowned. "Everybody knows about the Starbuck fortune. Why, even in an out-of-the-way place like Medicine Lodge I don't suppose there's a dozen people who haven't heard about your father, and most of the people there have also heard of you."

"I suppose you intended to flatter me," Jessie told him coldly. "You don't."

"I don't feel any need to flatter a prisoner," Caldwell snapped. His voice was hard with anger now.

"Release me, then," Jessie suggested mockingly.

"After the trouble I've taken to capture you?" he snapped. "Don't make the mistake of taking me for a fool!"

"I wouldn't be making a mistake by doing that," Jessie said in a quiet, sober voice. "Only a fool would waste a heritage such as the one your father left you."

"Leave that old bastard out of it!" Caldwell snapped. "He didn't leave me a thing but a bank I didn't like and didn't want. A bank still burdened with debt after he ran it for twenty years!"

"Such as the loan my father made him?" Jessie suggested.

"That, and a lot more! Alex Starbuck had plenty, more than anybody had a right to! Now you've got what he had, and I don't plan to put my money with it! In my book, money's made to spend and enjoy."

Jessie made no reply to Caldwell's remark. She'd

achieved what she'd set out to do. From her first encounter with Blaise Caldwell she'd sensed that there was something wrong with him. Now his words and actions had convinced her that she'd been captured by a lunatic whose irrational thoughts and actions were uncontrollable and unpredictable.

Caldwell waited for a moment, his face wrinkling into a scowl as Jessie remained silent. When he saw that she was not going to answer, he went on, "Too bad I was wrong about you, Miss Starbuck."

"Wrong?" Jessie frowned. "In what way?"

"Why, I thought, if you got a little bit better acquainted with me, we might hit it off together. Join forces, you know. But I see now I made a bad mistake. We'll get to where we're going in a little while. I regret that it won't be Medicine Lodge. I'd hoped to have the pleasure of your charms in more comfortable surroundings, but you leave me no choice. But we'll be in adequate surroundings for Whitey and I have our fun. After that—I guess you can see—we don't have any choice but to get rid of you so you can't tell anybody about us."

As he'd done on his earlier surprise visit, Caldwell tapped on the top of the carriage. It slowed in response to his signal. He opened the door and leaped out. In a moment the carriage lurched into motion again, leaving Jessie to rack her brain trying to find a solution to her even more precarious situation.

Ki finished his scanty meal before he'd covered a great deal of distance from the fork where he turned onto the almost-unused and long-abandoned southeastern branch of the old army road. The few bites that had been left in Jessie's saddlebags did not draw his attention from the landau's wheel-marks. The ruts were much easier to follow now, for while wagon-tracks had been plentiful between Dodge City and the fords across the Arkansas, they'd become more and more scarce on the trace he now followed.

Here the ruts were no longer intertwined in an almost undecipherable pattern, and the job of following the landau's track became simpler. Ki's spirits lifted after his few bites of food took effect and were kept high by the greater ease he had in keeping an eye on the trail. Now for the first time he had an opportunity to intensify his efforts in planning Jessie's rescue.

He summoned up a half-dozen schemes, but he had to abandon each one because at some point he realized that all of them lacked some key element of the foreknowledge he needed to make any of them work. The most important of the missing bits of information was the time element involved. At the moment, Ki did not have the ghost of an idea of when he might expect to overtake the landau.

There was no way for him to know how many minutes or hours had passed between Jessie being captured and her leaving the hotel. He did not know when she'd been put into the landau, when the carriage had left Dodge City, or how fast it was capable of moving.

As hard as he racked his brain, Ki could not come up with an equation or other sort of mathematical jugglery that would enable him to calculate the amount of time he'd lost by moving at the slow speed required prior to his first picking up the landau's trail at the ford. At last he gave up and concentrated on following the vehicle's wheel-ruts.

Even Ki's normally steadfast spirits faded as the sunlit sky ahead darkened and began to take on the hues of twilight. He watched with uncharacteristic impatience as the glow of sunshine diminished in the sky. He still had not overtaken the landau. In the east what had been a glowing sunlit arch of light blue was beginning to take on the deeper hue of nightfall when he met the first wagon he'd encountered on the almost-unused road. This time, Ki was the first to rein in and wait for the approaching wagon. He was both surprised and gratified when he saw that the teamster on the high wagon-seat was going to pull up beside him.

"Evening, stranger!" the man called as he reined to a creaking halt.

"Good evening," Ki nodded. "I suppose you're on the way to Dodge City?"

"Yep. And just might be the last time I head for there. Hell's bells, friend, I ain't got enough stuff in this wagon to pay me for hauling to Dodge."

"Shipping's slow now, I take it?"

"Slower'n a half-froze snail in wintertime. And that's just the half of it. I ain't one bit certain that I'm gonna be able to pick up a good load in Dodge to haul back. All the damn railroads git the business these days. It sure don't pay to run wagon-freight the way it used to when I fust got started at it."

"I've noticed how deserted this road's been since I turned onto it below the Arkansas bend," Ki replied.

"It sure don't amount to much these days," the man nodded. "Why, I usta meet ten, twelve wagons along this fork here. Now, look at you. You ain't pushing a team, and I'm damned if you ain't the only traveler I've run into since I passed a couple a stuck-up dudes in a fancy city rig back aways. At least you got sense enough to stop and swap hellos."

"You could tell they were city dudes?"

"Well, I jest reckon I could! Both of 'em was all dolled

up in fancy outfits, settin' on that high seat them landaus has got, lookin' down their noses at me! Why, they acted like they was too good to stop and swap a word or two with me!"

"Would that be a brown landau?" Ki asked.

"You seen 'em, too?"

"No. But I hope to see them very soon. How far back did you pass them?"

"Oh, a couple of hours, I'd say, six or eight miles." The teamster paused long enough to shoot a stream of brown tobacco juice on the ground, then frowned and went on, "You a friend of theirs?"

"No, but I think I know who they are," Ki said non-committally. "You're sure of what you said, that it's been two hours since you passed them?"

"Give or take a few minutes. You seem right pushed to catch up with 'em, if they ain't friends."

"I have some business to settle with them."

"Well, you ain't got on no fancy outfit, and you're Chinee to boot, but at least you got sense enough to stop and swap a hello with a man. Damn city dudes oughta stay in town!"

"Perhaps they should," Ki nodded. "But from what you've told me, I'll have quite a few more miles to go to catch up with that landau, and darkness is setting in. I must go on."

"Sure. I hope you make it where you're going all right."

"And I wish you the same," Ki nodded as he toed his horse ahead.

Assured now that Caldwell and his crony were only a short distance ahead of him, Ki felt free to speed up even at the risk of blowing the horses. As yet they showed no signs of fatigue in spite of the fast pace at which he'd kept them most of the day, but he knew well that the animals must be near the borderline where the long day's exertions would overtake them.

Even so, Ki toed the horse he was riding to an even faster pace. He kept his eyes fixed on the road in front of him, hoping that the men he was pursuing would either reach their destination or be forced to stop to rest the horse pulling the landau. As long as the carriage kept moving, he knew that Jessie would be safe.

Ki glanced at the sky. Its luminescence was fading fast. In a few minutes the last reflected rays of sunshine would be gone from the heavens. He turned his eyes to the small rolling hills that still dominated the landscape. He could still make out their contours, but the pin oaks that grew on them in scattered patches were blackly opaque in the growing gloom.

All the will Ki could summon was needed now to stop him from prodding the horses to a faster pace. Suddenly he straightened up, and then started swaying in the saddle as his own horse missed a step. It stumbled forward, almost fell. That was all the warning Ki needed. He reined in and dismounted, moved to Jessie's horse and mounted it. Then he started the animals moving once more.

Though the exchange had required only a few moments, even such a brief pause had given new life to the horse he'd ridden most of the day. Ki breathed a bit more easily after he'd gone another hundred yards and the horse that was now being led showed no signs of faltering. He glanced at the sky and saw that the last rays of sunshine had vanished from the heavens.

When he turned his eyes back to the road, Ki saw the first evidence of how little distance now separated him from the landau. A line of manure droppings such as a

160

moving horse voids was dotted along the dusty road just ahead. As he passed them, Ki could see that the small dark mounds were still glistening with moisture, and he knew that only minutes—at most a quarter of an hour—could have elapsed since they'd been dispelled.

Resisting the temptation to prod the tiring horses into a fresh burst of speed, Ki began searching the gloom that was gathering ahead. He knew he had little hope of overtaking the landau before darkness hid it from sight, but he was hoping that he would catch up with his quarry before Jessie's captors had a chance to harm her.

Jessie had rarely felt as alone as she did during the few, but seemingly long, minutes that passed when the landau slowed and the relative smoothness of the road gave way to a short period of lurches and bumps. She'd been in ranch wagons when they'd pulled off a road or beaten trail and started across open country, and she realized at once what the short rough passage signified.

Chafing mentally at her helplessness, bound tightly as she was, she still flashed defiance from her eyes at Blaise Caldwell when he opened the carriage door. He carried a lighted lantern, and Jessie blinked into the unaccustomed light after her long confinement in the curtained dimness of the landau.

Caldwell was grinning wolfishly in the yellow lantern light, which caught his eyes and seemed to magnify them. He said, "Well, Miss Starbuck, or perhaps I should call you Jessica now. After all, we've been fellow travelers most of the day. But you must be a bit tired and cramped after our long ride. We've reached our temporary destination now. But I'm afraid that for you it will be permanent."

★

Chapter 14

"Where are we now?" Jessie asked. "I don't see any lights around, so we can't be in a town. And it's impossible for us to've traveled far enough today to be in Medicine Lodge."

"An excellent guess," Caldwell replied. "But I won't spoil your surprise by filling in any details that your guesswork might have missed. Everything will be clear to you soon enough."

Jessie had no illusions about Blaise Caldwell. After his remarks to her during the day she'd started suspecting that he was insane. Several times his words had carried the twisted sort of or the backward-working logic that she knew often came from the minds of the insane or from those who were balancing precariously on the border between sanity and madness.

His actions during the long day's trip in the landau had also revealed his condition. His pointless visits, the manner in which he'd veiled her face so that she would be unable to see him, and his constant repetitive chatter had all been indications that, at the kindest judgment, Caldwell's mind was irrational. It was growing more and more obvious to her now that his brain did not function as did the minds of those who were well-balanced.

Before she could make any comment or reply to Caldwell's cryptic remark, Jessie saw a light suddenly flash in the darkness a short distance from them. The light grew brighter as it took the outline of a window.

"A house? Here?" she asked. She made no effort to conceal her surprise.

"Of course," Caldwell nodded.

"Yours?" Jessie frowned.

"Why, certainly. I'm sure you can understand that under the present circumstances I wouldn't care to stop at a place that belonged to someone else."

"I imagine you use it as a stopping place when you make one of your trips to Dodge City?"

"Since it doesn't really matter, I don't mind telling you," Caldwell nodded. "That's exactly right. Or, when I'm in a mood to entertain a lady such as yourself, Miss Starbuck."

"Where exactly are we, then?" Jessie went on. "I don't see the lights of a town anywhere."

"As I've told you before, I'm not exactly a fool," he said. "But since you're curious and telling you certainly won't do me any harm in the future, I don't object to explaining. We're about halfway between Dodge and Medicine Lodge."

"But why would you need a house—" Jessie stopped short, nodded and went on, "Of course. I think I understand now. The house and land really belong to the Medicine Lodge Bank."

"A good guess. And quite a correct one. The man who built the house died before the loan could be cleared and my father foreclosed on the mortgage, since the dead man had no heirs and still owed more than half of what he'd borrowed."

"Then when you inherited the bank, I suppose you discovered the mortgage and took the house over as a convenient place for your own activities?"

"Very shrewd, Miss Starbuck," Blaise agreed. "I'd almost forgotten that you inherited some banks from your father and are familiar with such things as mortgages and foreclosures. But I'm sure that Whitey's had time to put things in order. I didn't take time to clean the place up the last time I stopped here, but that's beside the point. Shall we go inside now and get better acquainted?"

"Do you intend to carry me, or will you untie my feet?"

Caldwell did not bother to reply. He took a penknife from his pocket and sawed at the rope that pinioned Jessie's ankles. It dropped away and she leaned forward, lifted her feet from the floor to stretch and rotate them for a moment until the feeling returned to them.

Then, because she'd realized after the conversations she'd had with Caldwell that she had no alternative but to be submissive and wait until she saw an opportunity to break free, Jessie stood up. With her wrists still bound, she bent forward, found her footing on the stirrup-step, and dropped lightly to the ground.

Ki fell back on the Oriental philosophy he'd been taught in childhood, the belief that what is destined to be will be. Though he still worried constantly about Jessie's welfare, he had accepted the fact that there was nothing he could do to lift the deepening darkness. He continued pushing steadily ahead, though at a somewhat slower pace.

Logic told him that there was no way the landau could have continued moving. The earlier gloom through which he'd been traveling was no longer that of a prolonged twilight. It had deepened to the full impenetrable darkness of night. It was unrelieved by any shred of brightness except the faint glow of stars, for the moon was in the beginning of its dark phase and would not rise until much later.

He'd also found that neither of the rented horses had been night-broken. They moved more slowly now no matter how often he prodded his toes into the flanks of the one he was astride. The led horse was much worse than the one Ki straddled. It tossed its head, occasionally loosed a shrill echoing neigh of protest, broke stride now and then, and once had started to bolt.

Although Ki had his full share of patience, he also had a cool and logical mind. Reason told him that Jessie's troubles would not vanish with the day, but would increase with the night. Determinedly, he calmed the horses as best he could when they grew restless and continued his slow progress along the deteriorating road that now was almost invisible.

"Welcome to my humble retreat, Miss Starbuck," Blaise Caldwell said mockingly as he opened the door and motioned for Jessie to go in first.

Jessie had no choice but to step inside. While Caldwell was securing the door-latch she looked around the room. It was almost square, with a door in the wall opposite the one where Jessie stood. The room was very sparsely furnished. Centered on the carpetless floor was a table with three or four chairs around it. An oil lamp with an unshaded glass chimney glowed from the middle of the table, otherwise its top was bare.

A battered rusting cookstove stood in a corner at the back of the room, its pipe running up through the roof. Near the stove a set of three shelves had been fixed to the wall; they contained an assortment of pots, pans, and thick earthenware plates and cups, and Jessie also caught the glint of a small heap of table utensils.

In the corner opposite the stove a narrow single bed stretched along the wall. It was more cot than bed, pillowless and covered with a crumpled blanket. Set into the side-wall above the bed there was the open window from which Jessie had seen the light glowing. She stood a pace or so from the door, inspecting the room. Meanwhile, Caldwell moved to the window and closed its shutters, securing them with a hook-eye.

"I'm afraid you won't find the accommodations here as comfortable as the Dodge House," Caldwell told Jessie as he turned away from the window. "But we'll only be here for tonight, and perhaps part of tomorrow." Then he grinned wolfishly and added, "How long we stay is up to you, in one way, you know."

Jessie gazed at him steadily but made no reply. Before Caldwell could say anything more, the door in the side wall swung open and the man called Whitey came into the room.

Jessie had not gotten a really good look at him before, no more than a glimpse in the dim room of the whore's crib in Dodge and another glimpse as he had bustled her into the landau. She took her time examining him now, and she did not like what she saw.

Whitey's appearance told Jessie all that she needed to

know about him. From his fuzzy grey derby hat and thick straggling black eyebrows to his over-full moustache with waxed upcurled ends and his checkered shirt and wide-striped pants and patent-leather shoes, he was typical of the breed of petty—and not so petty—criminals that had sprouted during the years that followed the Civil War.

Some had been army deserters moving west to evade capture. Some had belonged to the old gangs that were broken-up when the draft began and whose members had waited until the end of the conflict to move away from the crowded, well-policed eastern cities. A few were lawmen turned renegades, and Jessie put Whitey into this class. His beefy face, light grey eyes slitted by puffy lids, his square protruding chin, and his pock-scarred face spoke their own language. And that language translated into one word: trouble.

"If we're going to have any supper, we'll have to bring the victuals in from the rig," he told Caldwell. "But I got to admit I'd rather have that bottle of Green Valley that's in the grub-box than I would anything else."

"Bring the box in, then," Caldwell replied. "I'd like a sip of that Green Valley myself. And perhaps if I untie Miss Starbuck's hands, she could be persuaded to join us."

"Don't count on me joining you willingly for anything," Jessie said. Her voice was cold, and her words came out flatly, showing neither fear nor anger.

"It sounds like we'll have some taming to do," Caldwell commented, turning to Whitey.

"She sure wouldn't be the first one. You better leave her hands tied up till we got her tamed, though."

"I understand that the taming is part of your pleasure," Caldwell nodded. "Go get the liquor, Whitey. And you might as well unhitch the horse while you're out there.

Miss Starbuck and I can have a little chat while you're gone."

After Whitey had disappeared through the door, Caldwell turned to Jessie and went on, "Your remark a moment ago was very disappointing to me, Miss Starbuck."

"In what way?" she asked, realizing that she might be about to witness another example of his mental instability.

"In the past few hours I've thought about your situation quite seriously," Caldwell replied. "From the manner in which you've conducted yourself, I'm convinced now that I'd find you much more useful if you were working with me than if you were dead."

Jessie managed to hide her amazement. Since time was her only ally, she knew she must use it wisely.

"Working with you in what way?" she asked. Then choosing her words carefully, she went on, "You certainly can't expect me to overlook the way you've treated me so far."

"All that can be forgotten," Caldwell said. "We could—" He broke off as Whitey returned, carrying a bulky parcel.

"Let's have a drink, Blaise," Whitey said. "Then we can get things going like we've talked about. Now that we're here, there ain't no use to lallygag around. I'll lock the dame up in the other room, you and me can eat a bite and have a drink or two. Then we can start having our fun."

Ki had held himself back from pushing the horses into a race with total darkness after his encounter with the old freighter. Even with the certain knowledge that the landau he was after was the quarry he'd been seeking, he had no idea how much farther he might have to go in his pursuit of the pair who'd abducted Jessie and even less of an idea how he would free her.

Darkness had completed its conquest of daylight, and now Ki realized that even if he'd not been forced to hold to a slower pace when traveling through the gloom, the condition of the seldom-used road would have slowed his progress. As he pushed steadily ahead, he discovered that the road was not a great deal harder to follow than it had been in daylight. He soon found that he could maintain almost the same speed in the darkness that was possible during the sunlit hours.

Then at last he saw a dot of bright yellow gleaming ahead. Realizing that the glow might mark his objective, Ki kept the horses to their same careful pace. As he drew closer, the small yellow gleam took the rectangular form that identified it as a window, and Ki's caution increased.

He reined his mount to an even slower pace. Though it seemed to be a long time, less than a quarter of an hour lapsed before Ki reached a point where he could see the window clearly. He could also make out the vague outline of a small house or cabin in the thin feeble nimbus that radiated from the lamp-lit window. That was the point at which Ki reined in.

Dismounting, he led the horses through the deep gloom that prevailed to the edge of the arc of lamplight that spilled from the window. While he was tethering the animals, Ki jumped with surprise when light suddenly flooded the darkness.

Involuntarily, Ki took a step toward the silhouetted form of the man who was outlined by the bright light emitting from the opened door, but he stopped short when he realized the risk he might be taking by starting an attack without scouting. It occurred to him that there might be more men in the cabin than the two he'd been pursuing, and that Jessie might come to harm as the result of a premature attack. He continued his advance, but moved more slowly and with greater care.

At the edge of the dimness, Ki stopped. He watched with breath-bated silence while the man who'd come out begin to unhitch the horse. Counting on the man's attention being fully occupied for a few moments, Ki decided that he could reach the cabin safely. Keeping an eye on the man working at the landau, Ki bent low and dodged through the darkness *ninja* style until he reached the deep shadow of the cabin's wall.

There Ki dropped flat and wriggled along in the area of deepest darkness, at the base of the wall while he watched the man finish his unhitching job. Hiding the oval of his face with his black-sleeved forearm, Ki saw the man tether the horse to the landau's rear wheel and take a bulging flour sack out of the vehicle's boot.

Freezing in his position and stretching out flat against the wall in the black pool of darkness below the window, Ki watched the man carry the sack to the house. He heard Caldwell greet Whitey and heard the first few words of Whitey's response before the door closed.

When Ki felt it was safe for him to stand up and peer through the window, he shielded his face again with the sleeve of his jacket. Now that the stillness of the night had settled over the deserted landscape around the cabin he could hear the voices of those inside it faintly but quite clearly through the thin glass of the windowpane.

Now Ki heard Whitey say, "I'll lock the dame up in the other room, you and me can eat a bite and have a drink or two. Then we can start having our fun."

"Perhaps Miss Starbuck would like to stay and join us," Caldwell suggested.

"No, thank you," Jessie broke in.

Her voice through the glass sounded thin but the firmness in its tone was unmistakable to Ki.

"Damn it, Blaise! We didn't bring the woman out here to talk to!" Whitey told Caldwell. "We stopped here to get rid of her before we go on to Medicine Lodge! Don't forget, we just got till daybreak to do what we want to with her before we kill her."

"I'm not forgetting anything," Caldwell replied. "But I'm not like you, Whitey. I'd rather have her willing than fighting me all the time."

"Hell, that's half the fun of it!" Whitey replied. "Now, I know you're the boss and all that, but if you don't feel like taking her on soon as we've had a drink, I'll go first. And by the time I get finished breaking her in, you won't have any trouble getting her to do anything you want!"

"No!" Caldwell replied quickly. "We'll stick to our original plan!"

"Let's get started, then!" Whitey told him. "If you want her half-drunk and easy to handle, I'll hold her while you pour some of this Green Valley down her."

"You don't have to do that," Blaise replied. "But let's lock her in the other room while we have a drink and a bite to eat. While we're eating we can go over what I've got in mind for us to do when we get to Medicine Lodge."

"Oh, hell!" Whitey snorted. "We got all day tomorrow to do that, while we're going the rest of the way there. Right now I want to put my mind on a drink and a bite to eat and what I'm going to do when I get with the Starbuck woman."

For a moment Ki thought that Caldwell was going to

protest, but he finally settled with a shrug of agreement.

"Go ahead and put her in the other room, then," Ki heard Caldwell say. "Come to think of it, I could use a drink myself."

Ki waited only long enough to see Whitey start toward Jessie before he dropped his head below the level of the window and took a step aside from it. Safe now from any risk of being seen by the men inside, he started edging along the wall of the little cabin.

He reached the corner of the little building and turned to move along the end wall just as light flared through a window in the wall. Sure that the light must be coming from the room into which Whitey was taking Jessie, he hurried to the window and peered carefully inside.

He was just in time to see Whitey replacing the glass chimney of the lamp he'd lighted. Jessie was standing in the center of the small room and Ki noticed that her hands were bound. She was standing beside a narrow bed that, with a chair and the wash-stand on which the lamp rested, constituted the room's furnishings. Ki was ready to duck down when Whitey blew out the match he'd been holding and turned to Jessie.

"You better rest while you got the chance," Whitey told her. His voice was faint, filtering as it was through the glass pane, but Ki could hear him distinctly. He could also hear Jessie's reply.

"Yes," she told the outlaw. "I'll need my strength to fight both you and Caldwell. Don't worry. Whatever you've got in mind, I won't make it easy for you."

"We've handled fighting dames before now," Whitey boasted. "If push comes to shove, I don't expect we'll have much trouble with you."

Before Jessie could reply, Whitey turned and left the

172

room. Ki wasted no time. He tapped lightly on the windowpane with his fingertips. Jessie turned to look at the window for the first time. She opened her mouth, but before she spoke she closed it again as she shook her head.

Ki nodded his understanding of her silence. He began to run his hands along the window frame, seeking a weak spot where he could insert the edge of one of the *shuriken* he carried in his vest pocket. He found none, and seeing that Jessie had been watching him, shook his head.

Jessie moved to the window. She glanced at it and shook her head, then while Ki watched she sat down on the wash-stand, pulled her feet under her thighs and levered herself up. When she was standing on the little cabinet, she leaned forward and closed her hands over the long stout section of a peeled tree limb that had been wedged in between the upper edge of the lower sash and the window's top casing-board.

Ki tried the window again, and it opened readily. He began raising the sash, moving slowly to avoid making any noise. By this time Jessie had lowered herself to a sitting position on the wash-stand, she stood up and leaned out.

Ki wrapped his arms around her and helped her to the ground. "I'll cut the rope on your wrists as soon as we get to the horses," he whispered as he lowered her to the ground beside him. "There's no time to spare now."

Jessie nodded and gestured for Ki to move. Side by side they ran through the night, Ki leading the way to the place where he'd tethered the horses.

★

Chapter 15

Neither Jessie nor Ki spoke as they raced through the night. They'd covered perhaps a hundred yards in their flight from the cabin when a loud shout sounded behind them.

"They've found out you got away," Ki said without breaking his stride.

"I knew we didn't have much time," Jessie replied. "But I hoped you'd be able to get this rope off my wrists."

"There wasn't time, then," he told her. "But I think it's safe to stop here for a minute. They'll search close to the cabin first."

They halted, and Ki took a *shuriken* from his leather vest. Using the razor-sharp tip of one of its triangular points he made quick work of severing Jessie's bonds. She began flexing her fingers, as the shouts from the cabin stopped for a moment, then began again, now much louder than before.

"It sounds to me like they've come out to hunt for you," Ki said. His voice was as calm as though they were sitting at supper on the Circle Star and he was asking Jessie to pass him a plate. As he spoke he tucked the *shuriken* back in his vest pocket.

"Yes. And now that they're outside, I'm going back and get my Colt," she told him.

"That's a foolish risk!" Ki exclaimed.

"Not in the dark. And we'll need that pistol if they catch up with us."

"Then I'll go after it," Ki told her. "Do you know where it is?"

"It was lying on the front seat of the landau the last time I saw it. I don't remember seeing it in the cabin."

"Wait here," Ki said. "I'll be back in a few minutes."

Retracing a familiar trail even in the darkness was no real problem to Ki. He did not make the mistake of running at full tilt through the brush, but picked his way without hesitation as he moved at a quick walk. He zigzagged to keep on the grassy ground between the brush-clumps, where he could move silently.

As he kept up his swift progress, the shouts from Caldwell and Whitey receded. By the yells they exchanged Ki judged them to be moving away from the cabin instead of in his direction, and he speeded up. He reached the edge of the clearing. Now the boxy shape of the landau was visible, and he angled toward it. The carriage-horse snorted as he approached, but this did not disturb him.

Hurrying across the little cleared space to the landau, he opened the door. Even in the dark interior he could see Jessie's Colt outlined on the light-colored leather of the forward seat. He leaned in, grasped the revolver, and started back. As he moved, picking his way as carefully as

175

possible between the clumps of brush, he heard Caldwell's voice raised in a shout.

"Where in hell are you, Whitey?"

From a greater distance, the answer sounded, "Over here! That damn bitch must've gone the other way, or we'd've heard her in all this brush!"

"I'll start back toward the cabin, then," Caldwell called. "When you catch up to me, we'll look in the other direction. She can't've gotten very far away!"

A renewal of the loud sounds of brush cracking and rustling came to Ki through the darkness. He moved faster now, knowing that Caldwell and Whitey would be moving now and that their own noise would cover the fainter sounds he was making. He also knew that he and Jessie must be in their saddles before the pair got to the dense brush-clump where he'd hidden the horses.

"Did you find it?" Jessie asked when Ki emerged from the screening undergrowth.

"Right where you said it'd be," he replied as he handed her the Colt.

"Then let's hurry and get to our horses, Ki. I suppose you heard them as clearly as I did."

"Yes. But searching the brush between here and the cabin will slow them down," Ki replied as he and Jessie began moving again.

Behind them they could hear the noises made by Caldwell and Whitey as they moved toward them, the crackling of underbrush as they floundered around, the exchange of yells as they called to one another. Sounds travel far in open country on a still night, and Jessie and Ki were making their share of noise. Every time they ran into a patch of dry undergrowth the rattling of its branches and twigs sounded loud in their own ears, but Jessie and Ki now had an advantage over the killers who were trying to find them.

On his way to the cabin, Ki had looked behind him frequently and noted in his mind the two outstanding features of the terrain visible in the darkness: a ghostly white blob created in the underbrush by the weather-stripped bleached shoots of a dead shrub and beyond it the shape of an unusually tall tree that rose above those around it and showed in silhouette against the star-bright sky.

Using these two memorized guideposts to keep him and Jessie on the shortest route to the spot where he'd tethered their horses, they reached their goal while Caldwell and Whitey continued to flounder around in the brush closer to the cabin.

"Are your hands still too stiff to hold the reins?" Ki asked her as they stopped beside the tethered mounts.

"No. The rope wasn't all that tight, and I've been working my fingers now and then to get back their feeling. I might not be able to shoot very accurately for a little while, but I can handle the reins all right."

"Let's start moving, then. If we walk our horses to the road we won't make half as much noise as Caldwell and his crony are making beating the brush for us."

"I'd like to settle scores with them right now," Jessie said. "But they'll be in Medicine Lodge sometime later tomorrow, and I can wait that long."

"We'll walk the horses to the road, then, and circle around away from the cabin. As soon as we're out of earshot, we'll go back to the road and head for Medicine Lodge."

"We'll have a good lead," Jessie nodded. "We can make our plans while we ride, after we're sure we're well ahead."

They mounted and started toward the road. As they

crossed it into the sheltering brush they could still hear the shouts of Caldwell and Whitey in the vicinity of the cabin. They did not make the mistake of breaking into a gallop, but walked the horses as they wound through the dry undergrowth.

Circling wide, Ki and Jessie left the shouts behind them. When the noises made by their antagonists faded and could no longer be heard, they angled back to the road and reined their mounts toward Medicine Lodge. Though they kept the horses at a fast walk, the thudding hooves on the packed earth of the trace did not keep them from talking.

"Blaise Caldwell boasted a bit too much, Ki," Jessie said as they forged steadily ahead in the darkness. "I'm sure it's just as we've suspected all along, he cleaned out the Medicine Lodge Bank's vault and safety deposit boxes."

"He'd have had enough time to do it," Ki frowned. "There was quite a long period after that hold up attempt when nobody was watching the bank, and he'd certainly have duplicate keys."

"He's insane, of course," Jessie went on. "And very dangerous. I saw him and listened to his talk enough to know that. He should be in an asylum where he can't harm anyone again."

"That's why you're anxious to be waiting for him in Medicine Lodge, then?"

"Certainly. And to find the money he's stolen. We'll get there before Caldwell and his hired killer. And I'm sure that between us we can set a trap they'll walk into."

Jessie was beginning to feel restless. During the two hours that had passed since she and Ki began their vigil they'd seen nothing to indicate that it would be time well-spent.

No one had come anywhere near their waiting-post, a small secluded arbor that stood on the expansive grounds of an imposing white house. The house rose in solitary splendor in the center of a wide expanse of drying grass on the outskirts of Medicine Lodge. The half-circle of a gravel driveway curved in front of the massive two-story building.

When Jessie and Ki had arrived in Medicine Lodge in mid-afternoon they'd made carefully phrased enquiries both at the hotel where they'd checked in and at the restaurant where they'd enjoyed their first real meal since leaving Dodge City. In both places they'd been assured that Blaise occupied the family mansion when he was in town.

"It's the only one of its kind in town, all right," Ki had commented when they got their first glimpse of the place. "But I guess Blaise's father felt that he had to live in a place that proved his bank was strong and solid."

"Bankers usually do," Jessie nodded. "But it's going to be an easy place to watch. There aren't any other houses or buildings close by, except the stables. And that little arbor beyond the house will give us a place to watch without being seen."

"Suppose we ride as close to the arbor as we can," Ki suggested. He was pulling Jessie's Winchester out of its saddle scabbard as he spoke. He handed her the rifle and went on, "I'll take the horses and tether them behind the stable. Then I'll come back and join you."

After Ki had rejoined Jessie, they'd settled back on the narrow board benches that were the only seating arrangement the arbor boasted. Both were still tired from their long trip and sleepless night. The baths they'd enjoyed at the hotel had taken up as much time as they felt they could spare before beginning their search for Caldwell. After finding out about the big house they'd ridden out to it at once, tethered their horses behind its big barnlike stable, and started their vigil. Almost three hours had passed since then, and the strain of waiting after their rough trip was beginning to tell.

"In spite of what they told us in town, I'm not as sure as I was earlier that this is the first place Blaise Caldwell will head for when he gets to Medicine Lodge, Jessie," Ki said. "We've been here an hour or more, and there's still no sign of him."

"It's hard to predict what someone like Blaise will do, Ki." Jessie frowned. "But in such a small town, it isn't very likely that he'd have another place to go."

"We'll stick it out, then," Ki said. "But there's always a possibility that he went back to Dodge City to look for us."

"Let's give him until dark," Jessie suggested. "If he doesn't show up by then, we can start back to Dodge and try to find him. We might even meet him on the road, but I still think we'd be better off waiting here."

They sat in silence for what seemed a long time, but was in fact little more than a half-hour. Then Jessie suddenly half-rose from the bench and said, "I think our patience is finally about to be justified, Ki. There can't be two landaus in this part of Kansas, but I couldn't say for sure that this is the one we've been watching for. Remember, I never did get a good look at the outside of it."

"I did," Ki told her as he turned to look down the street in the direction Jessie was gazing and saw the tan landau. Even at a distance he recognized it and went on, "Yes, that's the one we've been hoping to see. And that's the plug-ugly, Whitey, in the driver's seat. I imagine Blaise Caldwell is inside, probably asleep."

180

"I'd say the best time to take them is when they get out and start for the house," Jessie suggested.

"Of course," Ki replied unhesitatingly. "It'll be easier than letting them get inside."

"I'll stay here in the arbor, then," Jessie told him. "I don't think they'll notice me if I crouch down between these benches."

"And I'll circle around the back of the house. Whistle when you come out of the arbor, Jessie. I'll be in place by then. If they've got any sense, they'll see we've got them in a crossfire and give up."

"I wish I was equally sure they'll surrender, but let's try. Hurry, Ki, before they get too close."

Ki started at a run, bending low. He moved like shadow, *ninja* fashion, and reached the concealment of the mansion just as the landau was turning into the semicircular driveway. Jessie dropped to a sitting position inside the arbor and returned her attention to the carriage.

Whitey had reined up in front of the mansion by now and was climbing down from the vehicle's high seat. He opened the door and stuck his head and shoulders inside. When he backed away, Blaise Caldwell appeared and swung down to the wide stirrup-type step. He turned to face Whitey, and the two men began talking.

Jessie was too far from them to hear what they were saying, but their vehement gestures indicated that they were carrying on an argument of some kind. She waited for a moment, her attention divided between keeping an eye on Caldwell and Whitey and glancing at the corner of the mansion, looking for Ki.

She saw him at last, stepping into the open space between the landau and the house. Rising to a kneeling position, holding her rifle butt to her shoulder ready to bring it up, she called to the two men at the carriage.

"Put your hands up and stand still!" she called. "I don't want to shoot. But if I have to, I'll shoot to kill!"

For a moment she thought that the two renegades were going to follow her orders, for they froze and Caldwell began to lift his arms. Then Whitey acted. He shoved Caldwell to the ground and started to run behind the landau.

Jessie was on her feet by now, heedless of the target she offered her antagonists. She raised her Winchester and let off a shot at the running desperado. He staggered but did not fall as her slug struck him.

Jessie was working the Winchester's loading-lever as she brought the rifle up and swung it to catch Caldwell in its sights. As she was tightening her trigger-finger a flashing silvery arc cut the air behind Whitey. Then Ki's *shuriken* buried itself in his throat.

When Jessie saw the *shuriken's* flash she held her fire. She watched Whitey as he broke stride. His hands were at his throat now, clawing at the points of Ki's throwing-blade that were embedded in his neck. Jessie was sure of Ki's skill with his *ninja* weapons and did not waste a shot. From the corner of her eye she saw Whitey begin to sag to the ground and turned her attention to Blaise Caldwell.

He had started a leap toward the open door when he saw his henchman fall, and Jessie fired without stopping to fine up her aim, a quick snapshot while she was still swinging the Winchester's muzzle. Caldwell's moving form jerked with the impact of the bullet, but he managed to half-fall, half-lurch into the landau's door, pulling his legs in after him.

Jessie levered another cartridge into the Winchester's chamber while Caldwell was moving, but before the lever locked the shell into place he was no longer visible. Then his revolver barked inside the landau, and the heavy lead slug whistled its shrill message of menace as it passed within inches of Jessie's ear before thunking into the latticework of the arbor and splintering the thin lath.

"Hold your fire, Jessie!" Ki warned. "But be ready to cut down on Caldwell if he shows himself! I'm going to move on the other side of the carriage!"

"Go ahead!" Jessie called in reply. "I'll be ready if he comes out."

Jessie could see the strip of withering grass that stretched between the landau and the mansion, but in his swift ground-hugging progress Ki had snaked halfway across it before she was positive that she'd spotted him. She watched him wriggling in quick swift sure moves toward the carriage, a shadow passing on the ground. Then he disappeared.

Standing tense, her rifle shouldered and ready for the pressure of the finger that she'd kept curled around the trigger, Jessie waited. She did not relax until she heard Ki's shout.

"Come on over here, Jessie!" he called. "Caldwell's got something he wants to tell you. Hurry up! He doesn't have much time left!"

Jessie lowered her Winchester and started at a run toward the landau. When she reached it she saw Ki standing in the open door on the other side of the carriage and Blaise Caldwell prone on the floor, his legs drawn up, his torso curled around them. She did not see the slowly growing puddle of blood that reddened the floor around him until she'd moved her eyes away from the wounded man's contorted face.

"Is there anything we can do to stop him from bleeding?" she asked Ki.

Shaking his head, Ki told her, "No. My *shuriken* cut his jugular vein. There's no way to stop it. Even if there was, it'd be too late."

Before Jessie could reply to Ki, Caldwell spoke. His voice was a rasping whisper. "Didn't start out . . . to give you trouble," he gasped. "Figured the bank . . . holdup . . . would cover me, but the damned fools . . . made too . . . many mistakes."

"You set up the robbery?" Jessie asked.

Caldwell's answering nod was feeble but positive.

"Where's the money from the bank, then?" she pressed, her voice urgent. "Tell me quickly! You don't have much time."

"Inside house here . . . in cellar," the dying man rasped. His voice had faded even more and Jessie had to lean forward to hear him as he went on, "Didn't mean . . . to start such . . ."

Caldwell's voice trailed off into silence, and his eyes seemed to bulge in their sockets as a final tremor shook him. Then he neither saw nor spoke nor moved.

"There's more than enough here to set the bank up again," Jessie told Ki. "And to pay off that old loan Alex made to Blaise Caldwell's father as well."

They were standing in the mansion's cellar. The door of the bricked vault they'd discovered behind a tier of shelves stood open, and its contents were spread across the floor.

"Is that what you plan to do?" Ki asked.

Jessie shook her head. "No. We'll stay here long enough to find the right people here in Medicine Lodge to get the bank going again. Then I'll turn it over to them."

"And I'm sure I can guess what you'll want to do then," Ki said.

"Of course you can, Ki. And I know that you'll be just as glad as I will to settle down for a long quiet rest at the Circle Star."